Pelican Books
Philosophy
Editor: Ted Honderich

What Sort of People Should There Be?

Jonathan Glover was born in 1941 and
was educated at Tonbridge School
and Corpus Christi College, Oxford.
He is a Fellow and tutor in philosophy
at New College, Oxford, and has
written *Responsibility* (1970) and
Causing Death and Saving Lives
(Pelican, 1977). He is married and
has three children.

D0874645

Jonathan Glover

What Sort of People Should There Be?

Penguin Books

Penguin Books Ltd, Harmondsworth, Middlesex, England
Penguin Books, 40 West 23rd Street, New York, New York 10010, U.S.A.
Penguin Books Australia Ltd, Ringwood, Victoria, Australia
Penguin Books Canada Ltd, 2801 John Street, Markham, Ontario, Canada L3R 1B4
Penguin Books (N.Z.) Ltd, 182–190 Wairau Road, Auckland 10, New Zealand

First published 1984

Copyright © Jonathan Glover, 1984
All rights reserved

Made and printed in Great Britain by
Richard Clay (The Chaucer Press) Ltd, Bungay, Suffolk
Filmset in Monophoto Photina by
Northumberland Press Ltd, Gateshead

Except in the United States of America, this book is sold subject
to the condition that it shall not, by way of trade or otherwise, be lent,
re-sold, hired out, or otherwise circulated without the
publisher's prior consent in any form of binding or cover other than
that in which it is published and without a similar condition
including this condition being imposed on the subsequent purchaser

To Daniel, David and Ruth

Contents

CONTENTS

Part Three: Values

Acknowledgements

I am grateful to many people who have helped with this book. I have discussed its topics with undergraduates and graduates at Oxford in classes and tutorials. I have also learnt from helpful disagreements and suggestions expressed in groups I have talked to in Oxford and in other universities and colleges.

Nancy Davis and Jeff McMahan each generously wrote penetrating comments on the book at an earlier stage, which have led to many changes for the better.

Among those I have learnt from in discussions of these issues over the last few years are Ruth Chadwick, Jeremy Cherfas, Ronnie Dworkin, Chris Graham, Jim Griffin, Dick Hare, John Harris, Ted Honderich, Richard Keshen, Richard Lindley, Derek Parfit, Joseph Raz, Don Regan, Alan Ryan, Amartya Sen, Wayne Sumner and Bernard Williams.

I owe a lot to Freddie Ayer, for stimulating my early interest in philosophy, and for much help and support.

Michael Dover, as Penguin editor, has always been most helpful, and has shown an astonishing patience with the gap between the original deadline and the arrival of the manuscript.

I am grateful to Vicky Banbury for typing much of the book, and to Sylvia Graham and Sylvia Barkwell for typing the rest.

Most of all, I have been influenced by my wife, Vivette. We have talked a lot about this book. She has sometimes, probably rightly, been a bit sceptical about parts of it. Reading it over, I notice how many passages, especially those about the kinds of world we should most hope for, are attempts to express things I have learnt from her.

Chapter 1 Introduction

This book is about some questions to do with the future of mankind. The questions have been selected on two grounds. They arise out of scientific developments whose beginnings we can already see, such as genetic engineering and behaviour control. And they involve fundamental values: these technologies may change the central framework of human life. The book is intended as a contribution, not to prediction, but to a discussion of what sort of future we should try to bring about.

1 The Questions

At one level, the questions fall into two groups. Some are about what we should do with genetic engineering. Perhaps one day we shall be able to choose people's genetic characteristics. How should we decide what sort of people there should be? Or are there reasons for refusing to make such decisions? The second group of questions is about the possible impact of technologies based on neurobiology, psychology and artificial intelligence. We may greatly increase our ability to alter people's experiences, and to control their motives and actions. We may develop far more powerful techniques for monitoring both behaviour and mental states. Such power to control and to understand people seems a threat to autonomy and to privacy. It may also threaten other things, such as our sense of identity, or the value we place on having relatively undistorted experience of the world as it really is. Other problems are raised by the development of machines able to duplicate or surpass our abilities and skills. Which activities should we keep for ourselves? What will the knowledge of our replaceability do to our way of seeing ourselves and what we do?

The issues raised by these possible future technologies are, at one level, very varied. But part of the argument developed here will be that, at another level, many of the same questions about our basic values recur in these different contexts. These central common themes are often lost sight of in the discussion of a particular topic, such as genetic engineering, where the shape of people's views is largely determined by what they think is likely to happen in practice. Perhaps by taking several topics it may be possible to show in clearer outline the central questions about values. These are questions about what human life should be like, and what sort of people there should be.

I have paid only rather limited attention to current beliefs about which technical developments are probable and which improbable. This is for several reasons. Predictions of that kind are usually short-term, and lose plausibility when extended beyond a decade or so. The time-span here is not intended to be limited to a few decades. Even in the short term, predictions of technical developments are often wrong: the atomic bomb exploded a decade after Rutherford ruled out the possibility of any practical application of atomic energy. And, because people, thought to be realistic, only believe developments are likely when they are nearly upon us, the time we have to think about what to do with discoveries is usually much too short. There is something to be said for taking a generous view of what may happen, so that we develop the habit of thinking about the best policy well in advance, rather than always too late.

Many people, when thinking of such possibilities as genetic engineering or techniques for controlling behaviour, have a reaction of rather inarticulate horror or revulsion. It is much easier to feel disturbed and repelled by these enterprises than it is to give a coherent account of precisely what the objections are. If we stay inarticulate, events will perhaps take one of two courses. The first is that the techniques will be adopted, in a piecemeal way, a little at a time. The advocates will at each stage be able to offer some specifiable gain, such as a reduction in the crime rate, or an increase in average intelligence, and each time this may seem more compelling than rather vaguely formulated objections on principle. By easy stages, we could move to a world which none of us would choose if we could see it as a whole from the start. Another possibility is that our resistance will prove too deeply rooted for all this, and that these techniques will fall under some general and undiscriminating ban. This will be a less disturbing outcome from our point of view, as the world will remain more as it is now. But the result may be that future generations will lose things they would have found of great value. Leaving the objections at the level of inarticulate opposition excludes the possibility of discriminating between desirable and undesirable applications of the new technologies.

These questions are worth thinking about only on certain assumptions. One is that we do have a future: that we will not die out because of shortages of food or energy, and that we will not destroy ourselves by war or by some other blunder. We cannot be certain that this assumption is correct. The avoidance of such disasters is our immediate problem, and one more urgent to think about than the questions of this book. But in thinking, as elsewhere, there is division of labour, and not everyone should concentrate on the most urgent questions to the exclusion of longer-term issues. And, if we do have a future, these questions about what sort of people there should be, which are starting to creep up on us now, will be more urgent themselves.

Another presupposition is that the future of the human race will be determined, at least in part, by what people decide. There is an obvious way in which this is true. Decisions to use or not to use genetic engineering in certain ways will make a difference to the composition of subsequent generations. But there are views according to which thinking about the sort of world we want is a waste of time, because what happens is determined by social or technological forces far more powerful than the values people have. Clearly the shape of society is not determined only by our thoughts and desires. Yet it is hardly plausible that our values have no impact at all on what the world is like. And, to the extent that we are able to choose between different futures, it is worth thinking about how desirable we find them.

About the questions discussed, I have the same thought that P. B. Medawar expressed about the questions of his Reith lectures on *The Future of Man*.[1] He said, 'I think that the answers to questions of this kind, in so far as it is possible to answer them, are deeply necessary for any understanding of the future of man; and when I say that they are necessary, please remember that I have not said, and do not imply, that they are sufficient.'

2 The Approach

The discussion falls into three parts. The first part is about genetic engineering. The second is about technologies related in one way or another to the brain. The third is about some general issues arising from the other parts.

1. *The Future of Man* (The Reith Lectures, 1959), London, 1960.

The discussion of genetic engineering has as a central theme the question of whether it is desirable to try to modify human nature. Genetic engineering seems a good test case for this question, as it seems to open up the possibility of more fundamental changes than we could otherwise envisage. Perhaps partly for this reason, it arouses in us kinds of resistance that go very deep. There are other issues discussed: whether genetic change is different in principle from environmental change; whether the distinction between remedying genetic defects and making genetic improvements is important; and problems about who should take decisions about genetic changes. But, important as these other issues are, the central issue is about changing human nature. I want to argue for greater willingness to consider policies that would do this, so it seems important to meet conservatism about human nature on its strongest ground. The aim of the discussion is to diagnose the varied sources of our resistance to genetic engineering, and to see how far they withstand scrutiny when separated. My hope is to give due weight to the legitimate sources of anxiety and resistance, and, by doing this, to detach them from what seems to me a misguided opposition in principle to any changes in our nature.

If we reject any general ban on changing human nature, it is then obviously important to think about the values to be used in deciding for or against any proposed change. The second part of the book, which is mainly about possible future technology applied to the brain, attempts to bring the relevant values into sharper focus. The aim is to apply to some of our values an approach Bertrand Russell spoke of in a quite different context. He said, 'The process of sound philosophizing, to my mind, consists mainly in passing from the obvious, vague, ambiguous things, that we feel quite sure of, to something precise, clear, definite, which by reflection and analysis we find is involved in the vague thing we start from, and is, so to speak, the real truth of which that vague thing is a sort of shadow.'[2]

The method to be used here for moving from the vague shadow to something more precise does not derive from Russell. It has been used throughout the history of philosophy since Socrates. The reader is presented with a series of thought experiments: in this case various technologies will be imagined in extreme forms. My responses will be given to these possibilities, in the hope that the reader too will have some responses.

2. *The Philosophy of Logical Atomism*, London, 1918, Lecture One.

I said earlier that little notice will be taken of which technical developments are thought probable (though none of the ones to be discussed is now known to be impossible). This will strike many as a serious weakness. On the conventional view, nothing is more damning than the criticism that some issue being discussed is based on assumptions that are 'unrealistic'. On this view, the way to think about issues like behaviour control is to avoid far-out science-fiction cases, and confine our thinking to the developments that, from our present perspective, seem likely. I hold the opposite view. In thinking about the desirability of various developments, it is often best deliberately to confront the most extreme possibility. Why is this?

Thinking about the desirability of different futures cannot be separated from thinking about present values. And our values often become clearer when we consider imaginary cases where conflicts can be made sharp. The complexity of practical detail, so essential to a decision in a particular context, has a softening and blurring effect when we are trying to think about what our priorities are in general. Also, if we consider 'moderate' rather than extreme cases, our judgements are often influenced by awareness of being on a slippery slope. Rather than the extreme development being fully ignored, it lurks unconfronted as the thought of some nameless horror further down the slope. Another feature of thinking only about what at the time seems likely, is that we are hardly ever able to choose between kinds of life in general. We are limited to piecemeal decisions. A series of incremental decisions can lead us somewhere we would never have chosen to go in the first place, and rule out places we might have done well to go to. Lack of realism is a serious criticism of practical proposals, such as an economic programme based on false factual assumptions. It is not a serious criticism of philosophical thought experiments about values, unless it is supposed that responses reflecting our real priorities can only be elicited by very familiar and homely kinds of cases. This is often asserted, but less often argued for.[3]

When Russell talked of moving from the vague, shadowy belief to something precise, he had in mind the philosophical analysis of common-sense beliefs of a quite uncontroversial kind, such as that the room he was lecturing in contained a number of people. But, in discussing values,

3. All the same, the reader should bear in mind a comment by Nancy Davis on an earlier draft of this book: 'I don't think that we can so easily suppose that our reactions are linear: that we can apply our reactions to sci-fi cases back to our mundane judgements.'

it is less obvious that there are agreed beliefs to start from. Some of the values that will figure prominently here might have meant little to a medieval European, and may mean little now to people in China or Japan. And even among the likely readers of this book, although I hope there will be understanding of its values, it would be unrealistic to expect general agreement.

The aim is to bring out some of the underlying questions of value more clearly. The intention is to describe possibilities in ways that separate out different values, and to say, 'these values, rather than those, are what matter, aren't they?' Of course, in a way I hope for the answer 'yes'. But, because people have different outlooks, the answer will quite often be 'no'. My hope is that those who answer 'no' will have been helped to see more clearly what it is they do not believe, and perhaps as a result to work out more fully what they do believe.

Some people hope for more than this from philosophical discussion of values. What they hope for, and what some philosophers attempt to provide, is a proof of the validity of one set of values, and a demonstration that others are mistaken. There is not room here to argue the matter, but I am sceptical of the possibility of this. It is a tempting fantasy for someone writing a book like this one to think that any reader who is rational and who understands the argument will be transformed into a person with the same views as the writer. However tempting, it is still a fantasy.

But there is a different way of seeing argument in ethics. Perhaps its social function is to spell out different sets of values more fully than they usually appear, so that people can accept or reject policies with greater awareness of the implications of their choices. This more modest function may still be worthwhile. For there is a danger that we will drift into a world much less good than we could have, as the result of making piece-meal, short-term decisions, rather than thinking coherently about kinds of life as a whole.

One stage of thinking about a possible future world is to ask ourselves what we like or dislike about it, and what reasons we have. This involves both judging that possible world by our own values, and critical reflection on those values themselves. For the reasons we give may turn out, when clearly stated, to be open to criticism. Objections to the conditioning techniques used in *Brave New World* invite the challenge to say just what it is that makes them worse than the more haphazard methods used in our own society. Perhaps this challenge can be met, but on the way we will be forced to do some fresh thinking about what autonomy is, and why we value it.

The third part of the book tries to place the discussion in a larger context. Suppose we are fairly clear about our own reasons for approving or disapproving of a particular kind of society. Many possible kinds of future world (Brave New World is one) come out badly in terms of some of our values, and yet would be highly rated by their inhabitants. Changes in society and in human nature can be expected to involve changes in values. So the next stage of thinking is to ask what we should try to do for future generations. Should we care at all what sort of people there are, a hundred years from now, and what their life is like? If we should, what is the role of our own attitudes in assessing ways of life in which those attitudes would no longer exist? One thought here is that, in deciding what we ought to do, there is no total escape from our own viewpoint. On the other hand, it seems parochial and constricting to take decisions about the future with only our own outlook in mind. Perhaps we should not give our own late-twentieth-century attitudes a privileged position? But, even if we decide to give weight to future attitudes we do not share, commitment to this degree of impartiality must be a feature of our own system of values. Here too, thinking about the future is a way of thinking about ourselves.

Part One: Genes

Chapter 2 Questions about Some Uses of Genetic Engineering

NOBEL 'SUPER BABIES'

Three exceptionally intelligent women have been fertilized from a sperm bank whose donors are all Nobel prize-winning scientists, the *Los Angeles Times* reported yesterday.

The babies, due this year, would be the first to result from a programme set up by a California businessman, Mr Robert Graham, aimed at producing people of superior intelligence, the newspaper said.

One of the sperm donors was Dr William Shockley, aged 70, who shared the Nobel prize for Physics in 1956, it was reported. Dr Shockley caused a minor sensation in the early 1970s when the US National Academy of Sciences refused to sponsor a study of his contention that human intelligence was mostly the result of heredity. He said that blacks scored on average about 15 points below whites in intelligence tests.

The newspaper quoted Mr Graham, aged 74, as saying that so far at least four Nobel prize-winners in addition to Dr Shockley had donated to the sperm bank. Apart from the three women who have been inseminated, more than a dozen have expressed interest in the idea, the newspaper said.

It said the existence of the sperm bank was confirmed by Dr Shockley and at least five other people. 'Yes, I'm one of them,' Dr Shockley was quoted as saying. He said he was disappointed that more of his fellow Nobel scientists had not been willing to add their names to what he called 'this good cause'.

GUARDIAN, 1 March 1980

Sir,

May I, as a citizen and a Nobel laureate, make a few comments on your front-page story ('Nobel Super Babies')?

The vast majority of Nobel laureates are scientists, most of them

23

specialists. They are not necessarily all of superior intelligence; they are primarily men and women who have been *successful* in a particular kind of intellectual endeavour, and people of comparable stature are to be found in large numbers in all walks of life.

As one of our foremost biologists, Sir Peter Medawar, has several times explained clearly, 'positive eugenics', i.e. breeding for the 'improvement' of the human species, is for many reasons not practicable. Even if Mr Graham's project is to be considered an experiment, it will never be possible to judge its results, since Nobel laureates are a very small sample even of the world's scientists.

As is now well known, the development of intelligence, as it is usually understood, is only partly controlled by heredity. At any rate, it is equally vital for success in life that a child grows up in a harmonious family and that he be offered the best possible opportunities for education.

By consenting to take part in Mr Graham's ill-considered project, the five Nobel laureates and the three women involved have raised doubts about their possession of the very asset they want to pass on to their offspring: intelligence.

Finally, I find it morally reprehensible and presumptuous for anybody to put himself forward as a judge of the qualities for which we should breed.

N. Tinbergen, in a letter to the *GUARDIAN*, 5 March 1980

Should we try to alter the genetic composition of future generations? Eugenic proposals, such as those of Mr Graham and Dr Shockley, have always aroused strong passions. Some hope that we can escape from our present innate limitations, and discard our less admirable qualities. Seen in this way, adopting a policy of deliberate genetic change would be a beneficial turning-point in the history of the human race. Others think of the abuses (perhaps remembering the Nazi experiment) and feel revulsion and dread at the horrors even a well-intentioned policy could lead to.

This debate, while confined to eugenics, has not been at the centre of attention, because of doubts about the workability of eugenic schemes. The debate will become less academic if we develop genetic engineering techniques to give us power directly to choose the genes of future people.

My concern, in the first part of this book, is to raise the question of how far, if at all, we should adopt policies designed to change human nature. I take the particular case of genetic engineering because it may provide the most extreme possibilities of this, and seems likely to arouse the deepest resistance. It poses the underlying issues with particular sharpness.

There is a widespread view that any project for the genetic improvement of the human race ought to be ruled out: that there are fundamental objections of principle. The aim of this discussion is to sort out some of the main objections. It will be argued that our resistance is based on a complex of different values and reasons, none of which is, when examined, adequate to rule out in principle this use of genetic engineering. The debate on human genetic engineering should become like the debate on nuclear power: one in which large possible benefits have to be weighed against big problems and the risk of great disasters. The discussion has not reached this point, partly because the techniques have not yet been developed. But it is also partly because of the blurred vision which fuses together many separate risks and doubts into a fuzzy-outlined opposition in principle.

1 Avoiding the Debate about Genes and the Environment

In discussing the question of genetic engineering, there is everything to be said for not muddling the issue up with the debate over the relative importance of genes and environment in the development of such characteristics as intelligence. One reason for avoiding that debate is that it arouses even stronger passions than genetic engineering, and so is filled with as much acrimony as argument. But, apart from this fastidiousness, there are other reasons.

The nature–nurture dispute is generally seen as an argument about the relative weight the two factors have in causing differences within the human species: 'IQ is 80 per cent hereditary and 20 per cent environmental' versus 'IQ is 80 per cent environmental and 20 per cent hereditary'. No doubt there is some approximate truth of this type to be found if we consider variations within a given population at a particular time. But it is highly unlikely that there is any such statement

25

which is simply true of human nature regardless of context. To take the extreme case, if we could iron out all environmental differences, any residual variations would be 100 per cent genetic. It is only if we make the highly artificial assumption that different groups at different times all have an identical spread of relevant environmental differences that we can expect to find statements of this kind applying to human nature in general. To say this is not to argue that studies on the question should not be conducted, or are bound to fail. It may well be possible, and useful, to find out the relative weights of the two kinds of factor for a given characteristic among a certain group at a particular time. The point is that any such conclusions lose relevance, not only when environmental differences are stretched out or compressed, but also when genetic differences are. And this last case is what we are considering.

We can avoid this dispute because of its irrelevance. Suppose the genetic engineering proposal were to try to make people less aggressive. On a superficial view, the proposal might be shown to be unrealistic if there were evidence to show that variation in aggressiveness is hardly genetic at all: that it is 95 per cent environmental. (Let us grant, most implausibly, that such a figure turned out to be true for the whole of humanity, regardless of social context.) But all this would show is that, within our species, the distribution of genes relevant to aggression is very uniform. It would show nothing about the likely effects on aggression if we use genetic engineering to give people a different set of genes from those they now have.

In other words, to take genetic engineering seriously, we need take no stand on the relative importance or unimportance of genetic factors in the explanation of the present range of individual differences found in people. We need only the minimal assumption that different genes could give us different characteristics. To deny *that* assumption you need to be the sort of person who thinks it is only living in kennels which makes dogs different from cats.

2 Methods of Changing the Genetic Composition of Future Generations

There are essentially three ways of altering the genetic composition of future generations. The first is by environmental changes. Discoveries in medicine, the institution of a National Health Service, schemes for poverty relief, agricultural changes, or alterations in the tax position of large families, all alter the selective pressures on genes.[1] It is hard to think of any social change which does not make some difference to who survives or who is born.

The second method is to use eugenic policies aimed at altering breeding patterns or patterns of survival of people with different genes. Eugenic methods are 'environmental' too: the difference is only that the genetic impact is intended. Possible strategies range from various kinds of compulsion (to have more children, fewer children, or no children, or even compulsion over the choice of sexual partner) to the completely voluntary (our present genetic counselling practice of giving prospective parents information about probabilities of their children having various abnormalities).

The third method is genetic engineering: using enzymes to add to or subtract from a stretch of DNA.

Most people are unworried by the fact that a side-effect of an environmental change is to alter the gene pool, at least where the alteration is not for the worse. And even in cases where environmental factors increase the proportion of undesirable genes in the pool, we often accept this. Few people oppose the National Health Service, although setting it up meant that some people with genetic defects, who would have died, have had treatment enabling them to survive and reproduce. On the whole, we accept without qualms that much of what we do has genetic impact. Controversy starts when we think of aiming deliberately at genetic changes, by eugenics or genetic engineering. I want to make some brief remarks about eugenic policies, before suggesting that policies of deliberate intervention are best considered in the context of genetic engineering.

Scepticism has been expressed about whether eugenic policies have any practical chance of success. Medawar has pointed out the importance of genetic polymorphism: the persistence of genetically different types in a population.[2] (Our different blood groups are a familiar example.) For many characteristics, people get a different gene from each parent. So children do not simply repeat parental characteristics. Any simple picture

1. Chris Graham has suggested to me that it is misleading to say this without emphasizing the painful slowness of this way of changing gene frequencies.

2. *The Future of Man* (The Reith Lectures, 1959), London, 1960, chapter 3; and in 'The Genetic Improvement of Man', in *The Hope of Progress*, London, 1972.

27

of producing an improved type of person, and then letting the improvement be passed on unchanged, collapses.

But, although polymorphism is a problem for this crudely utopian form of eugenics, it does not show that more modest schemes of improvement must fail. Suppose the best individuals for some quality (say, colour vision) are heterozygous, so that they inherit a gene A from one parent, and a gene B from the other. These ABs will have AAs and BBs among their children, who will be less good than they are. But AAs and BBs may still be better than ACs or ADs, and perhaps much better than CCs or CDs. If this were so, overall improvement could still be brought about by encouraging people whose genes included an A or a B to have more children than those who had only Cs or Ds. The point of taking a quality like colour vision is that it may be genetically fairly simple. Qualities like kindness or intelligence are more likely to depend on the interaction of many genes, but a similar point can be made at a higher level of complexity.

Polymorphism raises a doubt about whether the offspring of the three 'exceptionally intelligent women' fertilized by Dr Shockley or other Nobel prize-winners will have the same IQ as the parents, even apart from environmental variation. But it does not show the inevitable failure of any large-scale attempts to alter human characteristics by varying the relative numbers of children different kinds of people have. Yet any attempt, say, to raise the level of intelligence, would be a very slow affair, taking many generations to make much of an impact. This is one reason for preferring to discuss genetic engineering. For the genetic engineering of human improvements, if it becomes possible, will have an immediate effect, so we will not be guessing which qualities will be desirable dozens of generations later.

There is the view that the genetic-engineering techniques required will not become a practical possibility. Sir MacFarlane Burnet, writing in 1971 about using genetic engineering to cure disorders in people already born, dismissed the possibility of using a virus to carry a new gene to replace a faulty one in cells throughout the body: 'I should be willing to state in any company that the chance of doing this will remain infinitely small to the last syllable of recorded time.'[3] Unless engineering at the stage of sperm cell and egg is easier, this seems a confident

3. *Genes, Dreams and Realities*, London, 1971, p. 81.

dismissal of the topic to be discussed here. More recent work casts doubt on this confidence.[4] So, having mentioned this scepticism, I shall disregard it. We will assume that genetic engineering of people may become possible, and that it is worth discussing. (Sir MacFarlane Burnet's view has not yet been falsified as totally as Rutherford's view about atomic energy. But I hope that the last syllable of recorded time is still some way off.)

The main reason for casting the discussion in terms of genetic engineering rather than eugenics is not a practical one. Many eugenic policies are open to fairly straightforward moral objections, which hide the deeper theoretical issues. Such policies as compulsory sterilization, compulsory abortion, compelling people to pair off in certain ways, or compelling people to have more or fewer children than they would otherwise have, are all open to objection on grounds of overriding people's autonomy. Some are open to objection on grounds of damage to the institution of the family. And the use of discriminatory tax- and child-benefit policies is an intolerable step towards a society of different genetic castes.

Genetic engineering need not involve overriding anyone's autonomy. It need not be forced on parents against their wishes, and the future person being engineered has no views to be overridden. (The view that despite this, it is still objectionable to have one's genetic characteristics decided by others, will be considered later.) Genetic engineering will not damage the family in the obvious ways that compulsory eugenic policies would. Nor need it be encouraged by incentives which create inequalities. Because it avoids these highly visible moral objections, genetic engineering allows us to focus more clearly on other values that are involved.

(To avoid a possible misunderstanding, one point should be added before leaving the topic of eugenics. Saying that some eugenic policies are open to obvious moral objections does not commit me to disapproval of all eugenic policies. In particular, I do not want to be taken to be opposing two kinds of policy. One is genetic counselling: warning people of risks

4. 'Already they have pushed Cline's results further, obtaining transfer between rabbit and mouse, for example, and good expression of the foreign gene in its new host. Some, by transferring the genes into the developing eggs, have managed to get the new genes into every cell in the mouse, including the sex cells; those mice have fathered offspring who also contain the foreign gene.' Jeremy Cherfas: *Man Made Life*, Oxford, 1982, pp. 229–30.

in having children, and perhaps advising them against having them. The other is the introduction of screening-programmes to detect foetal abnormalities, followed by giving the mother the option of abortion where serious defects emerge.)

Let us now turn to the question of what, if anything, we should do in the field of human genetic engineering.

3 The Positive–Negative Distinction

We are not yet able to cure disorders by genetic engineering. But we do sometimes respond to disorders by adopting eugenic policies, at least in voluntary form. Genetic counselling is one instance, as applied to those thought likely to have such disorders as Huntington's chorea. This is a particularly appalling inherited disorder, involving brain degeneration, leading to mental decline and lack of control over movement. It does not normally come on until middle age, by which time many of its victims would in the normal course of things have had children. Huntington's chorea is caused by a dominant gene, so those who find that one of their parents has it have themselves a 50 per cent chance of developing it. If they do have it, each of their children will in turn have a 50 per cent chance of the disease. The risks are so high and the disorder so bad that the potential parents often decide not to have children, and are often given advice to this effect by doctors and others.

Another eugenic response to disorders is involved in screening-programmes for pregnant women. When tests pick up such defects as Down's syndrome (mongolism) or spina bifida, the mother is given the possibility of an abortion. The screening-programmes are eugenic because part of their point is to reduce the incidence of severe genetic abnormality in the population.

These two eugenic policies come in at different stages: before conception and during pregnancy. For this reason the screening-programme is more controversial, because it raises the issue of abortion. Those who are sympathetic to abortion, and who think it would be good to eliminate these disorders will be sympathetic to the programme. Those who think abortion is no different from killing a fully developed human are obviously likely to oppose the programme. But they are likely to feel that elimination of the disorders would be a good thing, even if not an adequate justification for killing. Unless they also disapprove of contraception, they are likely to support the genetic-counselling policy in the case of Huntington's chorea.

Few people object to the use of eugenic policies to eliminate disorders, unless those policies have additional features which are objectionable. Most of us are resistant to the use of compulsion, and those who oppose abortion will object to screening-programmes. But apart from these other moral objections, we do not object to the use of eugenic policies against disease. We do not object to advising those likely to have Huntington's chorea not to have children, as neither compulsion nor killing is involved. Those of us who take this view have no objection to altering the genetic composition of the next generation, where this alteration consists in reducing the incidence of defects.

If it were possible to use genetic engineering to correct defects, say at the foetal stage, it is hard to see how those of us who are prepared to use the eugenic measures just mentioned could object. In both cases, it would be pure gain. The couple, one of whom may develop Huntington's chorea, can have a child if they want, knowing that any abnormality will be eliminated. Those sympathetic to abortion will agree that cure is preferable. And those opposed to abortion prefer babies to be born without handicap. It is hard to think of any objection to using genetic engineering to eliminate defects, and there is a clear and strong case for its use.

But accepting the case for eliminating genetic mistakes does not entail accepting other uses of genetic engineering. The elimination of defects is often called 'negative' genetic engineering. Going beyond this, to bring about improvements in normal people, is by contrast 'positive' engineering. (The same distinction can be made for eugenics.)

The positive–negative distinction is not in all cases completely sharp. Some conditions are genetic disorders whose identification raises little problem. Huntington's chorea or spina bifida are genetic 'mistakes' in a way that cannot seriously be disputed. But with other conditions, the boundary between a defective state and normality may be more blurred. If there is a genetic disposition towards depressive illness, this seems a defect, whose elimination would be part of negative genetic engineering. Suppose the genetic disposition to depression involves the production of lower levels of an enzyme than are produced in normal people. The negative programme is to correct the genetic fault so that the enzyme level is within the range found in normal people. But suppose that within 'normal' people also. there are variations in the enzyme level, which correlate with ordinary differences in tendency to be cheerful or depressed. Is there a sharp boundary between 'clinical' depression and the depression sometimes felt by those diagnosed as 'normal'? Is it clear that a sharp distinction can be drawn between raising someone's enzyme level so that it falls within the normal range and raising someone else's level from the bottom of the normal range to the top?

The positive–negative distinction is sometimes a blurred one, but often we can at least roughly see where it should be drawn. If there is a rough and ready distinction, the question is: how important is it? Should we go on from accepting negative engineering to accepting positive programmes, or should we say that the line between the two is the limit of what is morally acceptable?

There is no doubt that positive programmes arouse the strongest feelings on both sides. On the one hand, many respond to positive genetic engineering or positive eugenics with Professor Tinbergen's thought: 'I find it morally reprehensible and presumptuous for anybody to put himself forward as a judge of the qualities for which we should breed.'

But other people have held just as strongly that positive policies are the way to make the future of mankind better than the past. Many years ago H. J. Muller expressed this hope:

And so we foresee the history of life divided into three main phases. In the long preparatory phase it was the helpless creature of its environment, and natural selection gradually ground it into human shape. In the second – our own short transitional phase – it reaches out at the immediate environment, shaking, shaping and grinding to suit the form, the requirements, the wishes, and the whims of man. And in the long third phase, it will reach down into the secret places of the great universe of its own nature, and by aid of its ever growing intelligence and cooperation, shape itself into an increasingly sublime creation – a being beside which the mythical divinities of the past will seem more and more ridiculous, and which setting its own marvellous inner powers against the brute Goliath of the suns and the planets, challenges them to contest.[5]

The case for positive engineering is not helped by adopting the tones of the mad scientist in a horror film. But behind the rhetoric is a serious point. If we decide on a positive programme to change our nature,

5. *Out of the Night*, New York. 1935. To find a distinguished geneticist talking like this after the Nazi period is not easy

this will be a central moment in our history, and the transformation might be beneficial to a degree we can now scarcely imagine. The question is: how are we to weigh this possibility against Tinbergen's objection, and against other objections and doubts?

For the rest of this discussion, I shall assume that, subject to adequate safeguards against things going wrong, negative genetic engineering is acceptable. The issue is positive engineering. I shall also assume that we can ignore problems about whether positive engineering will be technically possible. Suppose we have the power to choose people's genetic characteristics. Once we have eliminated genetic defects, what, if anything, should we do with this power?

The strategy of the discussion will be to separate out some different objections to positive engineering. In the next chapter some general issues of principle will be considered. The rest of this present chapter is about some more localized objections. There is the view that any benefit from a genetic improvement will be balanced by a related drawback. There are objections about damage to the family. There are criticisms of particular applications, such as cloning, or crossing species-boundaries. And there are objections to the risks involved, and to the possibility of mistakes.

4 The View That Overall Improvement is Unlikely or Impossible

There is one doubt about the workability of schemes of genetic improvement which is so widespread that it would be perverse to ignore it. This is the view that, in any genetic alteration, there are no gains without compensating losses. On this view, if we bring about a genetically based improvement, such as higher intelligence, we are bound to pay a price somewhere else: perhaps the more intelligent people will have less resistance to disease, or will be less physically agile. If correct, this might so undermine the practicability of applying eugenics or genetic engineering that it would be hardly worth discussing the values involved in such programmes.

This view perhaps depends on some idea that natural selection is so efficient that, in terms of gene survival, we must already be as efficient as it is possible to be. If it were possible to push up intelligence without

33

weakening some other part of the system, natural selection would already have done so. But this is a naive version of evolutionary theory. In real evolutionary theory, far from the genetic status quo always being the best possible for a given environment, some mutations turn out to be advantageous. and this is the origin of evolutionary progress. If natural mutations can be beneficial without a compensating loss, why should artificially induced ones not be so too?

It should also be noticed that there are two different ideas of what counts as a gain or a loss. From the point of view of evolutionary progress, gains and losses are simply advantages and disadvantages from the point of view of gene survival. But we are not compelled to take this view. If we could engineer a genetic change in some people which would have the effect of making them musical prodigies but also sterile, this would be a hopeless gene in terms of survival, but this need not force us, or the musical prodigies themselves, to think of the change as for the worse. It depends on how we rate musical ability as against having children, and evolutionary survival does not dictate priorities here.

The view that gains and losses are tied up with each other need not depend on the dogma that natural selection *must* have created the best of all possible sets of genes. A more cautiously empirical version of the claim says there is a tendency for gains to be accompanied by losses. John Maynard Smith, in his paper on 'Eugenics and Utopia',[6] takes this kind of 'broad balance' view and runs it the other way, suggesting, as an argument in defence of medicine, that any loss of genetic resistance to disease is likely to be a good thing: 'The reason for this is that in evolution, as in other fields, one seldom gets something for nothing. Genes which confer disease-resistance are likely to have harmful effects in other ways; this is certainly true of the gene for sickle-cell anaemia and may be a general rule. If so, absence of selection in favour of disease resistance may be eugenic.'

It is important that different characteristics may turn out to be genetically linked in ways we do not yet realize. In our present state of knowledge, engineering for some improvement might easily bring some unpredicted but genetically linked disadvantage. But we do not have to accept that there will in general be a broad balance, so that there is a presumption that any gain will be accompanied by a compensating loss

6. John Maynard Smith: *On Evolution*, Edinburgh, 1972; the article is reprinted from the issue on 'Utopia' of *Daedalus, Journal of the American Academy of Arts and Sciences*, 1965.

(or Maynard Smith's version that we can expect a compensating gain for any loss). The reason is that what counts as a gain or loss varies in different contexts. Take Maynard Smith's example of sickle-cell anaemia. The reason why sickle-cell anaemia is widespread in Africa is that it is genetically linked with resistance to malaria. Those who are heterozygous (who inherit one sickle-cell gene and one normal gene) are resistant to malaria, while those who are homozygous (whose genes are both sickle-cell) get sickle-cell anaemia. If we use genetic engineering to knock out sickle-cell anaemia where malaria is common, we will pay the price of having more malaria. But when we eradicate malaria, the gain will not involve this loss. Because losses are relative to context, any generalization about the impossibility of overall improvements is dubious.

5 The Family and Our Descendants

Unlike various compulsory eugenic policies, genetic engineering need not involve any interference with decisions by couples to have children together, or with their decisions about how many children to have. And let us suppose that genetically engineered babies grow in the mother's womb in the normal way, so that her relationship to the child is not threatened in the way it might be if the laboratory or the hospital were substituted for the womb. The cruder threats to family relationships are eliminated.

It may be suggested that there is a more subtle threat. Parents like to identify with their children. We are often pleased to see some of our own characteristics in our children. Perhaps this is partly a kind of vanity, and no doubt sometimes we project on to our children similarities that are not really there. But, when the similarities do exist, they help the parents and children to understand and sympathize with each other. If genetic engineering resulted in children fairly different from their parents, this might make their relationship have problems.

There is something to this objection, but it is easy to exaggerate. Obviously, children who were like Midwich cuckoos, or comic-book Martians, would not be easy to identify with. But genetic engineering need not move in such sudden jerks. The changes would have to be detectable to be worth bringing about, but there seems no reason why large changes in appearance, or an unbridgeable psychological gulf, should be created in any one generation. We bring about environmental changes which make children different from their parents, as when the first generation of children in a remote place are given schooling and made literate. This may cause some problems in families, but it is not usually thought a decisive objection. It is not clear that genetically induced changes of similar magnitude are any more objectionable.

A related objection concerns our attitude to our remoter descendants. We like to think of our descendants stretching on for many generations. Perhaps this is in part an immortality substitute. We hope they will to some extent be like us, and that, if they think of us, they will do so with sympathy and approval. Perhaps these hopes about the future of mankind are relatively unimportant to us. But, even if we mind about them a lot, they are unrealistic in the very long term. Genetic engineering would make our descendants less like us, but this would only speed up the natural rate of change. Natural mutations and selective pressures make it unlikely that in a few million years our descendants will be physically or mentally much like us. So what genetic engineering threatens here is probably doomed anyway.

6 Cloning

Cloning is reproduction of an organism by cell division. A cell-nucleus from the organism to be reproduced is transferred to an unfertilized egg whose own cell-nucleus has been removed. Where this is successful, the resulting organism has the same genetic make-up as the original one. If we develop techniques for cloning humans, should we use them?

If we think of producing a single offspring by cloning, there seems to be only one, rather speculative, objection. Perhaps there would be psychological problems, because of the special position of being a cloned offspring. (Scientists sometimes talk of the benefits to physics of being able to clone a replica of Einstein. If scientific originality depends less on genes than this project assumes, these expectations would create obvious problems for the less talented Einstein-clone.) But, if these problems are minor or non-existent, the production of a single cloned person seems unobjectionable.

When people are repelled by the thought of clones, they usually have in mind the creation of whole batches of people of identical composition.

This is unattractive because of the value we place on having a wide variety of different people. In an extreme case, where a town was entirely populated by one male clone and one female clone, there would be practical problems. (People might have problems telling who they were married to. And the police might find identification parades less useful.) But the practical drawbacks are not central. We feel our lives would be impoverished by the loss of variety. And our present degree of variety has genetic advantages. A very diverse gene pool makes it more likely that some of us will survive biological disasters such as the spread of some new and lethal disease.

We might expect cloning to change our relationships. Bernard Williams (in a different context) discusses what it would be like to love someone just as an instance of a type rather than as an individual person. He says,

We can dimly see what this would be like. It would be like loving a work of art in some reproducible medium. One might start comparing, as it were, performances of the type; and wanting to be near the person one loved would be like wanting very much to hear some performance, even an indifferent one, of Figaro – just as one will go to the scratch provincial performance of Figaro rather than hear no Figaro at all, so one would see the very run-down Mary Smith who was in the locality, rather than see no Mary Smith at all.[7]

These engaging thoughts about this disturbing possibility might never be actualized, because of the extent to which a relationship between two people depends on a history of shared experiences, and of their responses to each other. Perhaps cloning will alter relationships less than we might first think. (I wonder what it is like now to love someone who has an identical twin?) And any changes of a disturbing kind might be matched by compensating advantages. Members of a clone might develop special bonds of closeness and empathy.

It is hard to guess how far cloning would change relationships, or whether any changes would be on balance for better or worse. The central objections have to do with the narrowing of the gene-pool, and the impoverishing uniformity involved. These objections are so strong that any substantial use of cloning batches of people could only be justified by some very pressing reason, of a kind not now apparent.

7. 'Are Persons Bodies?', in *Problems of the Self*, Cambridge, 1973, p. 81.

7 Crossing Species Boundaries

Many people feel a revulsion at the thought of genetic engineering being used to produce creatures which would combine characteristics of more than one species, and feel this particularly strongly where one of the species in such a combination would be our own.

One reason for the revulsion may be the thought that the creature would be an outcast, not accepted as a member by the species from which it had come. But this is not the central reason. That could be dealt with by producing enough of the new type for them to make their own community.

More fundamental is the fear that inappropriate parts of different species could be combined. We think of a creature with a fair amount of human mentality unable to express much, because of the limitations of a body derived from a wolf or a cat. Perhaps we are influenced by stories like Kafka's *Metamorphosis*, where a man one day finds he has the body of an insect. This is a misleading way of thinking of what genetic mixing of species would be like, as a lot of the special horror of Kafka's story comes from the man having thoughts and feelings which depend on his having previously been an ordinary human. A better model of what inappropriate mixing might be like may be imprinting, where, for instance, young geese are given an early environment which gives them later a sexual orientation towards humans.

It is likely that we would only mix species if the resulting animals were going to have qualities that we would find useful. This suggests the purpose would only be exploitation. But this does not distinguish the genetic mix from other animals that we rear for purposes of exploitation. It is objectionable where our treatment of animals means that they have less good lives than they could have, but exploitation is not worse because the breed is an artificial product. Perhaps the special unpleasantness of combining exploitation with genetic mixing is in the possibility that creatures might be partly human. We imagine someone breeding a slave species combining the passive subservience of domesticated animals with some human intellectual skills.

The horror of the half-human slave species has two components. The first aspect of its awfulness is the probably unsatisfactory life of such creatures. It seems likely that the combination of such different genes would lead to psychological stresses and frustrations. And, if we suppose that genetic engineering has reached a level of precision where these conflicts can be eliminated, we may still feel, from our external perspective, that the life of these creatures is impoverished. The objection is not on grounds of misery or frustration, as these have been eliminated, but on grounds of possibilities that *we* can see have been lost: the possibilities in a fully human life. The objection is like that to some project of breeding contented mental defectives as slaves. They may be contented, and not miss lost aspects of life which they cannot understand. But we think it wrong to bring into the world people with such relatively impoverished lives when we could have brought normal people into the world instead.

The question of how we can be justified in thinking one sort of life more worthwhile than another is a central issue in this book. This is its first appearance, and here I just assume that many readers share the above view about breeding contented mental defectives. Some theoretical issues underlying such judgements are discussed in the last part of the book.

But, even if we are quite confident that contented creatures combining features of humans and of, say, cows have lives that are less worthwhile than fully human lives are, there is another problem. We say that, by adding some cow genes, we have produced sub-humans rather than humans. But someone might reply that, by adding some human genes, we have produced super-cows rather than cows. If the number of humans stays constant, and the population of ordinary cows declines as farmers choose to have super-cows instead, it is hard to see that the world has grown worse.

Yet, even if a particular project of mixing genes from different species involves no suffering, and even if we are persuaded by the 'super-cow' argument that the project involves no loss in quality of life, we may still feel repelled. Our revulsion has a second component, more to do with our own psychological needs than with the interests of the creature produced. Mary Douglas, in her anthropological theorizing, has stressed the importance to us of the main categories we use in classifying the world, and the disturbance induced by things that straddle or blur the boundaries between them. One of her illustrations of this is the idea of dirt:

It is a relative idea. Shoes are not dirty in themselves, but it is dirty to place them on the dining-table; food is not dirty in itself, but it is dirty to leave cooking utensils in the bedroom, or food bespattered on clothing; similarly, bathroom equipment in the drawing-room; clothing lying on chairs; outdoor things indoors; upstairs things downstairs; underclothing appearing where overclothes should be, and so on. In short, our pollution behaviour is the reaction which condemns any object or idea likely to confuse or contradict cherished classifications.[8]

She suggests that this point is relevant to the explanation of food taboos of the kind laid down in Leviticus, where some animals are thought unclean. Another example she gives of the importance of such boundaries applied to animals is in the outlook of the Lele:

Most of their cosmology and much of their social order is reflected in their animal categories. Certain animals and parts of animals are appropriate for men to eat, others for women, others for children, others for pregnant women. Others are regarded as totally inedible. One way or another the animals which they reject as unsuitable for human or female consumption turn out to be ambiguous according to their scheme of classification. Their animal taxonomy separates night from day animals; animals of the above (birds, squirrels and monkeys) from animals of the below: water animals and land animals. Those whose behaviour is ambiguous are treated as anomalies of one kind or another and are struck off someone's diet sheet. For instance, flying squirrels are not unambiguously birds nor animals, and so they are avoided by discriminating adults.[9]

When and how much people are disturbed by things anomalous in their system of classification is not an easy question. But, if we feel sympathetic to Mary Douglas's idea, its application to genetic mixing of the species will seem plausible. For the divisions between the species are the lines of *our* system of classifying animals, and disturbance at the thought of blurring them may be playing a part in our hostile response. And the division between our own species and others is even more important to our system of thought. Perhaps it was this, as well as religious belief, that motivated the resistance to Darwin.

To the extent that our resistance to genetic mixing is caused by revulsion against anomalies, it is tempting to dismiss it. Perhaps it is no more capable of rational justification than the food taboos of the Lele, and is something we could give up without loss. Some people hate the thought of intermarriage between races, and those of us who do not have that revulsion do not feel we lack anything of value. The temptation to dismiss our resistance as an irrational taboo is one we should mainly yield to. But some qualifications are necessary.

8. *Purity and Danger*, London, 1966, p. 48.
9. ibid. pp. 196-7.

It may not be easy to give up our feelings of revulsion. There seems little problem when we think in terms of other people giving up their food taboos. But, when we turn to our own, the psychological difficulty is clearer. If the most efficient meat production was the rearing of cats or rats for food, we might find our resistance hard to overcome. And the same might be true of our resistance to genetic mixing of species. We know rather little about how deep this kind of reaction goes, and should not assume that shedding taboos is without psychological cost.

Another qualification has to do with the effects of making traditional category boundaries seem less important by blurring them. Our present practice is to act in quite different ways towards humans and towards members of other species. We exploit animals for our food and our research, treating them in ways we would not think of treating even the most subnormal human being. If, instead of there being a clear gap between monkeys and ourselves, genetic mixing resulted in many individuals varying imperceptibly along the continuum between the two species, this might undermine our present belief in the moral importance of the distinction. If it did, the effects might go either way. There might be a beneficial reform in our attitudes towards members of other species. Or there might be a weakening of the prohibitions that now protect weaker or less intelligent humans from the treatment animals are subjected to. If the second possibility is a real danger, there is a strong case for resisting the blurring of this boundary.

8 Risks and Mistakes

Although mixing different species and cloning are often prominent in people's thoughts about genetic engineering, they are relatively marginal issues. This is partly because there may be no strong reasons in favour of either. Our purposes might be realized more readily by improvements to a single species, whether another or our own, or by the creation of quite new types of organism, than by mixing different species. And it is not clear what advantage cloning batches of people might have, to outweigh the drawbacks. This is not to be dogmatic that species mixing and cloning could never be useful, but to say that the likelihood of other techniques being much more prominent makes it a pity to become fixated on the issues raised by these ones. And some of the most serious objections to positive genetic engineering have wider application than to these rather special cases. One of these wider objections is that serious risks may be involved.

Some of the risks are already part of the public debate because of current work on recombinant DNA. The danger is of producing harmful organisms that would escape from our control. The work obviously should take place, if at all, only with adequate safeguards against such a disaster. The problem is deciding what we should count as adequate safeguards. I have nothing to contribute to this problem here. If it can be dealt with satisfactorily, we will perhaps move on to genetic engineering of people. And this introduces another dimension of risk. We may produce unintended results, either because our techniques turn out to be less finely tuned than we thought, or because different characteristics are found to be genetically linked in unexpected ways.

If we produce a group of people who turn out worse than expected, we will have to live with them. Perhaps we would aim for producing people who were especially imaginative and creative, and only too late find we had produced people who were also very violent and aggressive. This kind of mistake might not only be disastrous, but also very hard to 'correct' in subsequent generations. For when we suggested sterilization to the people we had produced, or else corrective genetic engineering for *their* offspring, we might find them hard to persuade. They might like the way they were, and reject, in characteristically violent fashion, our explanation that they were a mistake.

The possibility of an irreversible disaster is a strong deterrent. It is enough to make some people think we should rule out genetic engineering altogether, and to make others think that, while negative engineering is perhaps acceptable, we should rule out positive engineering. The thought behind this second position is that the benefits from negative engineering are clearer, and that, because its aims are more modest, disastrous mistakes are less likely.

The risk of disasters provides at least a reason for saying that, if we do adopt a policy of human genetic engineering, we ought to do so with extreme caution. We should alter genes only where we have strong reasons for thinking the risk of disaster is very small, and where the benefit is great enough to justify the risk. (The problems of deciding when this is so are familiar from the nuclear power debate.) This 'principle of caution' is less strong than one ruling out all positive engineering, and allows room for the possibility that the dangers may turn out to be very remote, or that greater risks of a different kind are involved in *not* using positive engineering. These possibilities correspond to one view of the facts in the nuclear power debate. Unless with genetic engineering we think we can already rule out such possibilities, the argument from risk provides more justification for the principle of caution than for the stronger ban on all positive engineering.

9 The Objections So Far

It is a widely held view that positive genetic engineering should in principle be ruled out. This belief, when combined with the view that it is acceptable to use genetic engineering to remedy defects, depends upon a distinction that is not completely sharp. But, assuming that some such distinction can at least roughly be drawn, some of the arguments against any positive engineering have been criticized.

· The arguments designed to show that overall improvement is unlikely need not deter us. Some are difficulties for eugenic breeding policies, which need not apply to genetic engineering. Others appeal to a principle we need not believe in: that genetic gains will always be balanced by compensating losses.

The need to protect family relationships creates a presumption that any genetic change should be brought about gradually. But this point, like other arguments for caution, should be placed in the context of the genetic changes which are taking place anyway, sometimes as the unintended results of policies of ours.

The disadvantages of cloning batches of people create a presumption against that policy. Our resistance to crossing species boundaries may be largely irrational, though in the case of mixing human and other genes, there may be dangers in undermining our resistance.

But the dominating reason for caution about adopting positive human genetic engineering, as well as for gradualness if we do adopt it, is the risk of some irreversible disaster. Even this risk has only been interpreted here as justifying a principle of caution rather than a total ban. Like all the objections considered so far, it is a matter of setting losses or risks against any possible benefits. Because all these objections have been of this kind, they are all, from the theoretical point of view, relatively clear. They are in some cases important, but most of them raise few deep issues not already present in debates on other possibly hazardous technology, or in debates on large scale social changes. The set of problems which raises deeper issues centres round the question: if we adopt positive genetic engineering, who is in a position to decide what future people should be like?

Chapter 3 Decisions

Like everyone else, philosophers measure their personal emotional
responses to various alternatives as though consulting a hidden oracle.
That oracle resides deep in the emotional centres of the brain,
most probably within the limbic system . . .

E. O. Wilson: *On Human Nature*

Some of the strongest objections to positive engineering are not about
specialized applications or about risks. They are about the decisions
involved. The central line of thought is that we should not start playing
God by redesigning the human race. The suggestion is that there is no
group (such as scientists, doctors, public officials, or politicians) who can
be entrusted with decisions about what sort of people there should be.
And it is also doubted whether we could have any adequate grounds
for basing such decisions on one set of values rather than another.

This chapter is about the 'playing God' objection: about the question
'Who decides?', and about the values involved. I shall argue that these
issues raise real problems, but that, contrary to what is often supposed,
they do not add up to an overwhelming case against positive engineering.

1 Not Playing God

Suppose we could use genetic engineering to raise the average IQ by
fifteen points. (I mention, only to ignore, the boring objection that the
average IQ is always by definition 100.) Should we do this? Objectors
to positive engineering say we should not. This is not because the present
average is preferable to a higher one. We do not think that, if it were
naturally fifteen points higher, we ought to bring it down to the present
level. The objection is to our playing God by deciding what the level
should be.

45

On one view of the world, the objection is relatively straightforward. On this view, there really is a God, who has a plan for the world which will be disrupted if we stray outside the boundaries assigned to us. (It is *relatively* straightforward: there would still be the problem of knowing where the boundaries came. If genetic engineering disrupts the programme, how do we know that medicine and education do not?)

The objection to playing God has a much wider appeal than to those who literally believe in a divine plan. But, outside such a context, it is unclear what the objection comes to. If we have a Darwinian view, according to which features of our nature have been selected for their contribution to gene survival, it is not blasphemous, or obviously disastrous, to start to control the process in the light of our own values. We may value other qualities in people, in preference to those which have been most conducive to gene survival.

The prohibition on playing God is obscure. If it tells us not to interfere with natural selection at all, this rules out medicine, and most other environmental and social changes. If it only forbids interference with natural selection by the direct alteration of genes, this rules out negative as well as positive genetic engineering. If these interpretations are too restrictive, the ban on positive engineering seems to need some explanation. If we can make positive changes at the environmental level, and negative changes at the genetic level, why should we not make positive changes at the genetic level? What makes this policy, but not the others, objectionably God-like?

Perhaps the most plausible reply to these questions rests on a general objection to any group of people trying to plan too closely what human life should be like. Even if it is hard to distinguish in principle between the use of genetic and environmental means, genetic changes are likely to differ in degree from most environmental ones. Genetic alterations may be more drastic or less reversible, and so they can be seen as the extreme case of an objectionably God-like policy by which some people set out to plan the lives of others.

This objection can be reinforced by imagining the possible results of a programme of positive engineering, where the decisions about the desired improvements were taken by scientists. Judging by the literature written by scientists on this topic, great prominence would be given to intelligence. But can we be sure that enough weight would be given to other desirable qualities? And do things seem better if for scientists we substitute doctors, politicians or civil servants? Or some committee containing businessmen, trade unionists, academics, lawyers and a clergyman?

What seems worrying here is the circumscribing of potential human development. The present genetic lottery throws up a vast range of characteristics, good and bad, in all sorts of combinations. The group of people controlling a positive engineering policy would inevitably have limited horizons, and we are right to worry that the limitations of their outlook might become the boundaries of human variety. The drawbacks would be like those of town-planning or dog-breeding, but with more important consequences.

When the objection to playing God is separated from the idea that intervening in this aspect of the natural world is a kind of blasphemy, it is a protest against a particular group of people, necessarily fallible and limited, taking decisions so important to our future. This protest may be on grounds of the bad consequences, such as loss of variety of people, that would come from the imaginative limits of those taking the decisions. Or it may be an expression of opposition to such concentration of power, perhaps with the thought: 'What right have *they* to decide what kinds of people there should be?' Can these problems be side-stepped?

2 The Genetic Supermarket

Robert Nozick is critical of the assumption that positive engineering has to involve any centralized decision about desirable qualities: 'Many biologists tend to think the problem is one of *design*, of specifying the best types of persons so that biologists can proceed to produce them. Thus they worry over what sort(s) of person there is to be and who will control this process. They do not tend to think, perhaps because it diminishes the importance of their role, of a system in which they run a "genetic supermarket", meeting the individual specifications (within certain moral limits) of prospective parents. Nor do they think of seeing what limited number of types of persons people's choices would converge upon, if indeed there would be any such convergence. This supermarket system has the great virtue that it involves no centralized decison fixing the future human type(s).'[1]

1. *Anarchy, State and Utopia*, New York, 1974, p. 315.

This idea of letting parents choose their children's characteristics is in many ways an improvement on decisions being taken by some centralized body. It seems less likely to reduce human variety, and could even increase it, if genetic engineering makes new combinations of characteristics available. (But we should be cautious here. Parental choice is not a guarantee of genetic variety, as the influence of fashion or of shared values might make for a small number of types on which choices would converge.)

To those sympathetic to one kind of liberalism, Nozick's proposal will seem more attractive than centralized decisions. On this approach to politics, it is wrong for the authorities to institutionalize any religious or other outlook as the official one of the society. To a liberal of this kind, a good society is one which tolerates and encourages a wide diversity of ideals of the good life. Anyone with these sympathies will be suspicious of centralized decisons about what sort of people should form the next generation. But some parental decisons would be disturbing. If parents chose characteristics likely to make their children unhappy, or likely to reduce their abilities, we might feel that the children should be protected against this. (Imagine parents belonging to some extreme religious sect, who wanted their children to have a religious symbol as a physical mark on their face, and who wanted them to be unable to read, as a protection against their faith being corrupted.) Those of us who support restrictions protecting children from parental harm after birth (laws against cruelty, and compulsion on parents to allow their children to be educated and to have necessary medical treatment) are likely to support protecting children from being harmed by their parents' genetic choices.

No doubt the boundaries here will be difficult to draw. We already find it difficult to strike a satisfactory balance between protection of children and parental freedom to choose the kind of upbringing their children should have. But it is hard to accept that society should set no limits to the genetic choices parents can make for their children. Nozick recognizes this when he says the genetic supermarket should meet the specifications of parents 'within certain moral limits'. So, if the supermarket came into existence, some centralized policy, even if only the restrictive one of ruling out certain choices harmful to the children, should exist. It would be a political decision where the limits should be set.

There may also be a case for other centralized restrictions on parental choice, as well as those aimed at preventing harm to the individual people being designed. The genetic supermarket might have more oblique bad effects. An imbalance in the ratio between the sexes could result. Or parents might think their children would be more successful if they were more thrusting, competitive and selfish. If enough parents acted on this thought, other parents with different values might feel forced into making similar choices to prevent their own children being too greatly disadvantaged. Unregulated individual decisions could lead to shifts of this kind, with outcomes unwanted by most of those who contribute to them. If a majority favour a roughly equal ratio between the sexes, or a population of relatively uncompetitive people, they may feel justified in supporting restrictions on what parents can choose. (This is an application to the case of genetic engineering of a point familiar in other contexts, that unrestricted individual choices can add up to a total outcome which most people think worse than what would result from some regulation.)

Nozick recognizes that there may be cases of this sort. He considers the case of avoiding a sexual imbalance and says that 'a government could require that genetic manipulation be carried on so as to fit a certain ratio'.[2] He clearly prefers to avoid governmental intervention of this kind, and, while admitting that the desired result would be harder to obtain in a purely libertarian system, suggests possible strategies for doing so. He says: 'Either parents would subscribe to an information service monitoring the recent births and so know which sex was in shorter supply (and hence would be more in demand in later life), thus adjusting their activities, or interested individuals would contribute to a charity that offers bonuses to maintain the ratios, or the ratio would leave 1:1, with new family and social patterns developing.' The proposals for avoiding the sexual imbalance without central regulation are not reassuring. Information about likely prospects for marriage or sexual partnership might not be decisive for parents' choices. And, since those most likely to be 'interested individuals' would be in the age group being genetically engineered, it is not clear that the charity would be given donations adequate for its job.[3]

If the libertarian methods failed, we would have the choice between allowing a sexual imbalance or imposing some system of social regulation. Those who dislike central decisions favouring one sort of person over

2. op. cit., p. 315.

3. This kind of unworldly innocence is part of the engaging charm of Nozick's dotty and brilliant book.

others might accept regulation here, on the grounds that neither sex is being given preference: the aim is rough equality of numbers.

But what about the other sort of case, where the working of the genetic supermarket leads to a general change unwelcome to those who contribute to it? Can we defend regulation to prevent a shift towards a more selfish and competitive population as merely being the preservation of a certain ratio between characteristics? Or have we crossed the boundary, and allowed a centralized decision favouring some characteristics over others? The location of the boundary is obscure. One view would be that the sex-ratio case is acceptable because the desired ratio is equality of numbers. On another view, the acceptability derives from the fact that the present ratio is to be preserved. (In this second view, preserving altruism would be acceptable, so long as no attempt was made to raise the proportion of altruistic people in the population. But is *this* boundary an easy one to defend?)

If positive genetic engineering does become a reality, we may be unable to avoid some of the decisions being taken at a social level. Or rather, we could avoid this, but only at what seems an unacceptable cost, either to the particular people being designed, or to their generation as a whole. And, even if the social decisions are only restrictive, it is implausible to claim that they are all quite free of any taint of preference for some characteristics over others. But, although this suggests that we should not be doctrinaire in our support of the liberal view, it does not show that the view has to be abandoned altogether. We may still think that social decisions in favour of one type of person rather than another should be few, even if the consequences of excluding them altogether are unacceptable. A genetic supermarket, modified by some central regulation, may still be better than a system of purely central decisions. The liberal value is not obliterated because it may sometimes be compromised for the sake of other things we care about.

3 A Mixed System

The genetic supermarket provides a partial answer to the objection about the limited outlook of those who would take the decisions. The choices need not be concentrated in the hands of a small number of people. The genetic supermarket should not operate in a completely unregulated way, and so some centralized decisions would have to be taken about the restrictions that should be imposed. One system that would answer many of the anxieties about centralized decision-making would be to limit the power of the decision-makers to one of veto. They would then only check departures from the natural genetic lottery, and so the power to bring about changes would not be given to them, but spread through the whole population of potential parents. Let us call this combination of parental initiative and central veto a 'mixed system'. If positive genetic engineering does come about, we can imagine the argument between supporters of a mixed system and supporters of other decision-making systems being central to the political theory of the twenty-first century, parallel to the place occupied in the nineteenth and twentieth centuries by the debate over control of the economy.[4]

My own sympathies are with the view that, if positive genetic engineering is introduced, this mixed system is in general likely to be the best one for taking decisions. I do not want to argue for an absolutely inviolable commitment to this, as it could be that some centralized decision for genetic change was the only way of securing a huge benefit or avoiding a great catastrophe. But, subject to this reservation, the dangers of concentrating the decision-making create a strong presumption in favour of a mixed system rather than one in which initiatives come from the centre. And, if a mixed system was introduced, there would have to be a great deal of political argument over what kinds of restrictions on the supermarket should be imposed. Twenty-first-century elections may be about issues rather deeper than economics.

If this mixed system eliminates the anxiety about genetic changes being introduced by a few powerful people with limited horizons, there is a more general unease which it does not remove. May not the limitations of one generation of parents also prove disastrous? And, underlying this, is the problem of what values parents should appeal to in making their choices. How can we be confident that it is better for one sort of person to be born than another?

---

4. Decision-taking by a central committee (perhaps of a dozen elderly men) can be thought of as a 'Russian' model. The genetic supermarket (perhaps with genotypes being sold by TV commercials) can be thought of as an 'American' model. The mixed system may appeal to Western European social democrats.

4 Values

The dangers of such decisions, even spread through all prospective parents, seem to me very real. We are swayed by fashion. We do not know the limitations of our own outlook. There are human qualities whose value we may not appreciate. A generation of parents might opt heavily for their children having physical or intellectual abilities and skills. We might leave out a sense of humour. Or we might not notice how important to us is some other quality, such as emotional warmth. So we might not be disturbed in advance by the possible impact of the genetic changes on such a quality. And, without really wanting to do so, we might stumble into producing people with a deep coldness. This possibility seems one of the worst imaginable. It is just one of the many horrors that could be blundered into by our lack of foresight in operating the mixed system. Because such disasters are a real danger, there is a case against positive genetic engineering, even when the changes do not result from centralized decisions. But this case, resting as it does on the risk of disaster, supports a principle of caution rather than a total ban. We have to ask the question whether there are benefits sufficiently great and sufficiently probable to outweigh the risks.

But perhaps the deepest resistance, even to a mixed system, is not based on risks, but on a more general problem about values. Could the parents ever be justified in choosing, according to some set of values, to create one sort of person rather than another?

Is it sometimes better for us to create one sort of person rather than another? We say 'yes' when it is a question of eliminating genetic defects. And we say 'yes' if we think that encouraging some qualities rather than others should be an aim of the upbringing and education we give our children. Any inclination to say 'no' in the context of positive genetic engineering must lay great stress on the two relevant boundaries. The positive – negative boundary is needed to mark off the supposedly un-acceptable positive policies from the acceptable elimination of defects. And the genes – environment boundary is needed to mark off positive engineering from acceptable positive aims of educational policies. But it is not clear that confidence in the importance of these boundaries is justified.

The positive–negative boundary may seem a way of avoiding objection-ably God-like decisions, on the basis of our own values, as to what sort of people there should be. Saving someone from spina bifida is a lot less controversial than deciding he shall be a good athlete. But the distinction, clear in some cases, is less sharp in others. With emotional states or intellectual functioning, there is an element of convention in where the boundaries of normality are drawn. And, apart from this, there is the problem of explaining why the positive–negative boundary is so much more important with genetic intervention than with environmental methods. We act environmentally to influence people in ways that go far beyond the elimination of medical defects. Homes and schools would be impoverished by attempting to restrict their influence on children to the mere prevention of physical and mental disorder. And if we are right here to cross the positive–negative boundary, encouraging children to ask questions, or to be generous and imaginative, why should crossing the same boundary for the same reasons be ruled out absolutely when the means are genetic?

It may be said that the genes–environment boundary is important because environmentally created changes can be reversed in a way that genetically based characteristics can not. But this perhaps underrates the permanence of the effects of upbringing. It may be that the difference is at best a matter of degree. And it is also hard to believe that irreversibility can be our main objection to crossing the genes–environment boundary. In bringing up our children, we try to encourage kindness and generosity. Would we really stop doing this if we were so effective that cruelty and meanness became impossible for them? It is not clear that our concern to develop their autonomy requires keeping open *all* possibilities, at whatever cost to our other values.

Yet there remains an unease about positive policies of moulding people in one direction rather than another, however much they are already incorporated in our child-rearing, and however reluctant we would be to abandon them altogether. And the unease is intensified when the methods are genetic, perhaps because the changes are likely to be less reversible, and perhaps because they may be more extreme. It may be said that we do not see the human race from the God-like perspective that seems to be required for making these decisions. We have our values, but perhaps we ought to be modest about them. E. O. Wilson's speculation that intuitions about values have their basis in the limbic system might be right. If so, perhaps genetic engineering could alter the limbic system, and so alter the values by which people judge these issues. And this raises the question of what basis we have for saying that genetic changes are improvements.

The sceptical case has been strongly stated by Bernard Williams. He talks of a difficulty

about the basis of values on which these supposed improvements would be introduced. One would have to take the kind of standpoint in which one regarded as self-evident to oneself what the future of the human race should be, presuppose that you knew what the human race was here for, and take all the steps you could to make it reach that ideal goal. But it is not at all clear where one is supposed to get that knowledge or information from.[5]

Talk of 'knowledge' and 'information' sets the standard rather high, requiring the proponents of positive genetic engineering to have solved problems about objectivity in ethics which we do not expect people arguing other cases to have solved. But the point can be freed from this implication by being put as a question: on what basis can we decide between bringing into existence different types of people?

If we take decisions of this sort, we cannot but be guided by our own values (which would perhaps have been different had our limbic systems been different). But this is a feature of any moral or political decision. And it is not obvious that we are the best possible people in terms of our own values. People more generous, braver and less conformist than ourselves may be people we can recognize would be better than us. This need not commit us to some utopian blueprint about what the human race is for, but could be a matter of piecemeal genetic engineering. We take a view about what sort of people we prefer when we make decisions about schooling, without claiming to know what the human race is here for. And, as with educational decisions, decentralized choices at the genetic stage could lead to variety rather than uniformity.

There is, of course, a general problem about the basis of the values we bring to any decision. But it is questionable how far this is an argument against intervention to change what people are like, whether the means are genetic or environmental. Why should we assume that opting for the genetic status quo involves less commitment to a world view than opting for a change? And, if we are sure that some genetic changes would be for the worse, and so want to restrict the genetic supermarket, is

5. 'Genetics and Moral Responsibility', in A. Clow (ed.), *Morals and Medicine*, London, 1970.

it really plausible to say we have no basis for thinking some changes would be for the better? The scepticism seems unjustifiably selective.

If positive genetic engineering is to be justified, there must be benefits to outweigh the risks. And the benefits have to be even greater if centralized social decisions are taken, not merely to filter out certain parental initiatives, but positively to encourage the development of some characteristics. I have argued that there should be a presumption in favour of decentralized choices, which are more likely to preserve or increase variety than decisions taken from the narrow viewpoint of the members of some central body. But this is a presumption rather than an absolute ban on any central initiative. The chance of securing some great benefit, or of avoiding some great catastrophe, might justify overriding the presumption. It is hard to imagine being persuaded of the rightness of such a policy if adopted undemocratically or if imposed by coercion. But, even with a democratically chosen policy, using only persuasion or incentives, there is still the liberal resistance to government endorsement of some types of people as more desirable than others.

5 Changing Human Nature

Positive genetic engineering raises two issues. Could we be justified in trying to change human nature? And, if so, is genetic change an acceptable method? Most of us feel resistance to genetic engineering, and these two questions are often blurred together in our thinking. One aim of the discussion has been to separate the different sources of our resistance. Another has been to try to isolate the justifiable doubts. These have to do with risks of disasters, or with the drawbacks of imposed, centralized decisions. They need not justify total rejection of positive engineering. The risks are good reasons for extreme caution. The other drawbacks are good reasons for decentralized decisions, and for resisting positive genetic engineering in authoritarian societies. But these good reasons are quite separable from any opposition in principle to changing human nature.

The idea of 'human nature' is a vague one, whose boundaries are not easy to draw. And, given our history, the idea that we must preserve all the characteristics that are natural to us is not obvious without argument. Some deep changes in human nature may only be possible if we do accept positive genetic engineering. It is true that our nature is not determined entirely by our genes, but they do set limits to the sorts of people we can be. And the evolutionary competition to survive has set limits to the sorts of genes we have. Perhaps changes in society will transform our nature. But there is the pessimistic thought that perhaps they will not. Or, if they do, the resulting better people may lose to unreconstructed people in the evolutionary struggle. On either of these pessimistic views, to renounce positive genetic engineering would be to renounce any hope of fundamental improvement in what we are like. And we cannot yet be sure that these pessimistic views are both false.

Given the risks that positive genetic engineering is likely to involve, many people will think that we should reject it, even if that means putting up with human nature as it is. And many others will think that, quite apart from risks and dangers, we ought not to tamper with our nature. I have some sympathy with the first view. The decision involves balancing risks and gains, and perhaps the dangers will outweigh the benefits. We can only tell when the details are clearer than they are now, both about the genetic techniques and about the sort of society that is in existence at the time.

It is less easy to sympathize with opposition to the principle of changing our nature. Preserving the human race as it is will seem an acceptable option to all those who can watch the news on television and feel satisfied with the world. It will appeal to those who can talk to their children about the history of the twentieth century without wishing they could leave some things out. When, in the rest of this book, the case for and against various changes is considered, the fact that they *are* changes will be treated as no objection at all.

Part Two: Thought Experiments

To romance of the future may seem to be indulgence in ungoverned speculation for the sake of the marvellous. Yet controlled imagination in this sphere can be a very valuable exercise for minds bewildered about the present and its potentialities. Today we should welcome, and even study, every serious attempt to envisage the future of our race, not merely in order to grasp the very diverse and often tragic possibilities that confront us, but also that we may familiarize ourselves with the certainty that many of our most cherished ideals would seem puerile to more developed minds. To romance of the far future, then, is to attempt to see the human race in its cosmic setting, and to mould our hearts to entertain new values.

Olaf Stapledon: *Last and First Men*

Chapter 4 Transparency

A remote radio-communications system using belt transceivers is presently undergoing prototype testing. Systems of this type can monitor geographical location and psychophysiological variables, as well as permit two-way coded communication with people in their natural social environment. Probable subjects include individuals susceptible to emergency medical conditions that occasionally preclude calling for help (e.g. epilepsy, diabetes, myocardial infarctions), geriatric or psychiatric outpatients, and parolees. It is conceivable, for example, that convicts might be given the option of incarceration or parole with mandatory electronic surveillance.

Robert L. Schwitzgebel: *Emotions and Machines: A Commentary on the Context and Strategy of Psychotechnology*

During the last few years, methodology has been developed to stimulate and record the electrical activity of the brain in completely unrestrained monkeys and chimpanzees. This procedure should be of considerable clinical interest because it permits exploration of the brain for unlimited periods in patients without disturbing their rest or normal spontaneous activities.

José M. R. Delgado: *Journal of Nervous and Mental Disease* 1968

The development of electronic monitoring devices makes it possible for us to keep people under surveillance without locking them up in prison. We could largely replace prison by a system of keeping track of convicted criminals without restricting their movements. This thought can arouse both anxiety and optimism. The anxiety (when not about the effectiveness of such a system in restraining criminal activity) is about the invasion of privacy involved in such monitoring. The optimism comes from the thought that submitting to a monitoring system might be much less terrible than going to prison.

Advocates of monitoring systems use the argument that they would be more humane, and would be no more an invasion of privacy than prison. They suggest that we should try out monitoring for its effectiveness in preventing crime. If these systems turn out to be no more ineffective than prisons, it may seem that their supporters will have won the argument.

But it is a bit more complicated than this. Monitoring systems, just because they are less horrible to submit to than prison, may be resorted to more readily. Periods of monitoring might be much longer than prison sentences, and many more people might be monitored than are now sent to prison. We would then live in a society in which many had lost a lot of privacy. Perhaps social gains, such as a reduced crime rate and the abolition of prisons, would be thought great enough to outweigh this loss. But the issue is not a simple one, and the ways in which monitoring techniques could be developed and used have to be taken into account.

One obvious development is to monitor, not merely where people are, but also various of their physical states. Dr Schwitzgebel mentions some useful applications of this internal monitoring in the cases of people with conditions dangerous to themselves. The extension to sex offenders, and to people liable to do harm when drunk or in fits of rage, can easily be imagined. And, as techniques for recording the electrical and chemical activity of the brain grow more sophisticated, we can expect it to become possible to monitor physical and psychological states with increasing precision.

When we think of more finely tuned monitoring, which would cross the blurred boundary between physical and psychological states, we are likely to feel increasing anxiety at the potential for invasion of privacy. To many people it will seem obvious that any extension of monitoring to psychological states should be resisted. But it is worth scrutinizing what is often taken for granted, and asking what the reasons are for valuing privacy as we do. Would it really be so terrible if our feelings and thoughts could be monitored by other people? What would be lost in a world without privacy?

To pose this issue in its sharpest form, let us consider the extreme case, in which the neurosciences have developed to the point where, by monitoring the activity of a person's brain, others could know in some detail the contents of his mind.

1 Monitoring Thoughts

The idea that we could monitor thoughts in this way presupposes that different mental states are correlated with different states of the brain. This is the working assumption of much psychology and neurophysiology, but it is controversial. We cannot be certain what future scientific work will show, and we are probably in for many surprises before the brain is fully understood. Yet there is already much suggestive work showing that electrical stimulation of particular points of the cortex can evoke highly specific memories, or that seeing particular patterns involves the firing of specific neurons in the cortex. In the scientific context, the working assumption, even if by no means impregnable, seems plausible.

Some philosophers have argued that there could not exist comprehensive and detailed psychophysical laws, while others disagree. These arguments will not be gone into here. The plan is to consider the implications of a technology based on monitoring brain activity, with deliberate casualness about current opinions as to which way the neurosciences will develop.

But there is a question which cannot be shelved here. What does it mean to talk of monitoring someone's thoughts and feelings? In a way, we all know what it is to have thoughts, and in most cases it seems absurd to suggest that someone does not know what thought he is having. Yet, despite this, there is a real problem in saying what having a thought consists in. And this problem causes difficulty for the idea of monitoring thoughts.

What is the problem about thoughts? Some thinking is in words, but sometimes we have a thought not formulated in words, where, if we are aware of anything, it is perhaps only some image. When I am struck by the thought that I have forgotten to telephone for a taxi, it may be that no words cross my mind. Perhaps I simply have a mental picture of a taxi. In such cases, images do not just come to mind on their own, but come with an interpretation. If I tell someone else that I have a mental picture of a taxi, he will not know what thought I am having, though I may be in no doubt at all that my thought is about the phone call. This process of interpretation, which applies to words as well as images, is something we know almost nothing about. This is why psychological studies of thinking, which can tell us so much about the strategies people use for solving problems, have so far told us so little about what our ordinary 'background' stream of consciousness consists in.

61

Because the process of interpretation is so important, even where the thought has embodiment in words or images, someone monitoring simply those words or images passing through my mind will have an incomplete knowledge of what I am thinking about. We can imagine a device that would decode the brain's activity and project on to a screen images corresponding to those in the person's mind. (We might need two screens: one for experiences involved in seeing, and one for visual imagination.) Thoughts which take place in words could be reproduced on a soundtrack, and images which are not visual or auditory could be reproduced by similar devices. But it is much less clear what it would be to give public embodiment to the process of interpreting these words and images. For this reason it seems better to discuss monitoring only words and images. It has to be recognized that a technology letting us do this would not give us perfect knowledge of people's mental lives.

Let us suppose that these devices are developed, and that they are produced in conveniently portable form. You come into the room holding what looks like a small portable television. The next thing I know is that I hear coming from it the words that are running through my mind, and see my accompanying visual images on the screen. This technology will make people's minds largely transparent. Despite the problems about interpreting words and images, we will often have a fairly good idea of what others are thinking.

Will this be the end of privacy? In one way, the answer is clearly 'yes'. For, as the onion layers of privacy are peeled away, if there is a centre it must surely be the contents of the mind. But the machines so far described will leave us with an intermittent privacy of a kind. For, while the contents of a mind would always in principle be open to inspection, for much of the time it would not be under scrutiny. This is because of our limited powers of attention. Even with several thought-reading machines going at once, I could only attend to the thoughts of one or two people at a time. Some television enthusiasts have more than one set, so that they can watch programmes on different channels at the same time. The limitations on how far this could go are obvious. And, apart from problems of limited attention, most of us would want to spend most of the time doing other things, or thinking our own thoughts, and would probably not spend long tuned in to the minds of others. (Though artists and writers might find their thoughts constantly monitored by people doing courses about creativity.)

A society or a government determined to eliminate privacy could over-come these difficulties by developing a central monitor and memory store, where everyone's thoughts could be recorded and stored, so that they would be available for scrutiny when desired. At this point, systematic thought policing would be possible.

In our present world, governments and other organizations can destroy or hamper the freedom to express thoughts, but at least thought itself is always free. The introduction of thought-policing would make many people's lives scarcely worth living. It would also give governments complete power to block new ideas and social change, if only by killing or locking up people as soon as they had the ideas. Thought-policing is so appalling that there is a lot to be said for the view that work on developing thought-reading machines is immoral, merely because it helps to make it possible.

2 Transparency in a Free Community

Much of the horror of devices to make our minds transparent to others has to do with their uses in an authoritarian society. We are surely right to fear these potential uses, but some of our deepest anxieties about privacy come from other sources. This can be seen by a thought experiment in which we eliminate misuse by the authorities. Imagine a community of free and equal people. (It is not clear what this comes to, but imagine the nearest we can get in practice to an anarchist utopia.) Even here, the general availability of thought-reading machines can be seen as a terrible threat.

Why should we be disturbed if our thoughts become transparent to others? Some explanations that come to mind involve particular projects, or particular kinds of thought, which generate their own reasons for secrecy. If we are trying to give someone a surprise, bargaining with him, or trying to swindle or cheat him, the project will collapse if our thoughts are publicly available. A society transparent in this way will be one in which bargaining and swindling are impossible, which will no doubt have repercussions on our economy. But most of us will see little reason for being appalled. More personal anxieties are stronger. Some of our thoughts would seem discreditable, or at least embarrassing. Feelings of jealousy or resentment, sexual fantasies, or Walter Mitty daydreams of a self-flattering kind would all be sources of embarrassment. And, less selfishly, we are glad to keep some thoughts about other people secret so that we do not hurt them.

But these reasons, although psychologically powerful, may not go to the heart of the matter. They concern particular kinds of thoughts and feelings. We can imagine a society in which bargaining and swindling did not exist, and in which daydreams and sexual fantasies were no longer a matter for embarrassment. In that society, people might still feel a resistance to their mental lives being made transparent to others. There is a case for saying that the value of privacy depends on something deeper than the embarrassing or hurtful aspects of particular thoughts and feelings. It may be bound up with the nature of relationships, and with our sense of our own identity.

3 Relationships

On one view, the fact that we have an area of privacy is more important than which particular activities or thoughts are included in it. (This is suggested in a particularly perceptive discussion of these issues by Charles Fried.[1]) The claim is that privacy is necessary for different kinds of relationship. We choose how far to admit people to friendship or other relationships with us partly by controlling how much of what is private we reveal to them. As Fried puts it,

Love or friendship can be partially expressed by the gift of other rights – gifts of property or of service. But these gifts, without the intimacy of shared private information, cannot alone constitute love or friendship. The man who is generous with his possessions, but not with himself, can hardly be a friend, nor – and this more clearly shows the necessity of privacy for love – can the man who, voluntarily or involuntarily, shares everything about himself with the world indiscriminately.

But is it certain that gradations of intimacy are necessary for differences of relationship? In a world of transparent relationships, there would still be room for people being generous with themselves to different degrees. We would continue to give people different amounts of our concern and our time. We would respond to people with varying degrees of warmth, and this would be more obvious than it is now. Close relationships would

1. *An Anatomy of Values*, Harvard, 1970, chapter 9.

consist in choosing to be together, and in the way people would feel about each other. There would no longer be the mutual lowering of the barriers of privacy. Closeness would be different from now, but not so different as to be non-existent.

It does seem that some of the pleasures of relationships involve talking about things that otherwise would be private. We like to do things together and to talk about our responses. (Part of the appeal of films and, especially, novels is that they often portray people from the inside, and so give us comparisons to use in trying to capture and articulate our own fugitive private experiences.) In talking to each other, and so learning to express (and sharpen) our experiences, we are doing something similar to what a novelist does. If we were transparent to each other, some of the things we now say would not need to be said. But it does not follow that all such conversation would be eliminated. This is because our conversation does not just report responses, but shapes them. We often only get clear about our *own* thoughts and feelings by trying to express them to someone else, and by listening to their thoughts in return. So transparency would not destroy conversation, though we might just think together without having to talk.

But another aspect of relationships might be threatened by transparency. In our present state, privacy gives a special quality to the times when it is waived. Other people can seem like medieval fortified towns. We can climb the hill and walk round outside their walls. But if they open the gate and let us in, we have the pleasures of exploration, seeing squares and houses and churches, sometimes like those we know and sometimes quite different. And while you are showing me round your town, I am showing you round mine, so that we are each at the same time explorer and host. A world without privacy would be a world in which the gates of all towns would always be open, so the excitement of the first admission would be less.

If these changes in relationships are for the worse, they provide a reason for rejecting, not only the thought-reading machine, but also any *voluntary* general lowering of the barriers which protect privacy. The changes are equally likely whether our privacy is invaded from outside or whether it is given away freely.

But the value placed on gradations of intimacy need not be a reason against a much greater degree of transparency than we have now. We hide behind so many different layers of defences. There are barriers created by context: you can't mention that here. And there are barriers of manner and style, created perhaps because we feel threatened, signalling that we are unapproachable about this, or will not talk about that. (Sometimes the threat turns out to be imaginary. Tolstoy describes this in *Anna Karenin*:

Levin had often noticed in discussions between the most intelligent people that after enormous efforts, and endless logical subtleties and talk, the disputants finally became aware that what they had been at such pains to prove to one another had long ago, from the beginning of the argument, been known to both, but that they liked different things, and would not define what they liked for fear of its being attacked. He had often had the experience of suddenly in the middle of a discussion grasping what it was the other liked and at once liking it too, and immediately he found himself agreeing, and then all arguments fell away useless. Sometimes the reverse happened: he at last expressed what he liked himself, which he had been arguing to defend and, chancing to express it well and genuinely, had found the person he was disputing with suddenly agree.[2]

When we do not feel threatened, we are more willing to take down the barriers, and less timid people sometimes take them down even when they do feel threatened.

It may be that already, as the result of innumerable individual decisions, we are moving towards greater transparency. These things are hard to establish, and no doubt vary from culture to culture. But it seems to me that in our century, there has been a strong trend towards greater honesty in relationships, with greater openness about things which used to be private, and that this is part of a beneficial transformation of our consciousness and social life. (If taking down the barriers is starting to transform us, the obstruction of this process is another charge, to add to the familiar ones, against political systems where people fear the authorities, and so need the barriers.) This change could go a long way further, and still leave us room for different degrees of privacy and intimacy.

The effects of transparency on relationships would be in several ways beneficial. Deception, with its resulting erosion of love and friendship, would be impossible. And relationships now are obscured, not only by deception, but also by our limited ability to express our thoughts and feelings, and by our lack of perception about other people. The thought-reading machine, because of the problems about interpretation, would

2. *Anna Karenin*, translated by Rosemary Edmonds, Harmondsworth, 1954, p. 421.

not abolish these limitations, but it would greatly reduce their obscuring effects. As we understood more about each other's mental lives, we would form more realistic pictures of each other, and it seems plausible that this would make relationships better rather than worse. And a stronger sense of community might result from the barriers of privacy coming down, together with the ending of a sense of loneliness and isolation which some people feel because of their inability to share their experiences.

Sometimes a society of transparent relationships is held up as an ideal. In a fine interview on his seventieth birthday,[3] Jean-Paul Sartre was asked, 'Does it bother you when I ask you about yourself?' He replied:

No, why? I believe that everyone should be able to speak of his innermost being to an interviewer. I think that what spoils relations among people is that each keeps something hidden from the other, something secret, not necessarily from everyone, but from whomever he is speaking to at the moment. I think transparency should always be substituted for what is secret, and I can quite well imagine the day when two men will no longer have secrets from each other, because no one will have any more secrets from anyone, because subjective life, as well as objective life, will be completely offered up, given ... There is an as-for-myself (*quant-à-soi*), born of distrust, ignorance, and fear, which keeps me from being confidential with another, or not confidential enough. Personally, moreover, I do not express myself on all points with the people I meet, but I try to be as translucent as possible, because I feel that this dark region that we have within ourselves, which is at once dark for us and dark for others, can only be illuminated for ourselves in trying to illuminate it for others ... One can't say everything, you know that well. But I think that later, that is, after my death, and perhaps after yours, people will talk about themselves more and more and that this will produce a great change. Moreover, I think that this change is linked to a real revolution. A man's existence must be entirely visible to his neighbour, whose own existence must in turn be entirely visible to him, in order for true social harmony to be established.

There is obviously a big difference between Sartre's ideal and the world of the thought-reading machine. Sartre envisages people voluntarily abandoning their own secrecy of thought, rather than having the power to invade that of others. His transition period would involve no loss of autonomy, and might involve relatively little distress. The introduction of the thought-reading machine would not respect people's autonomy, but would strip them of secrecy against their will. It is hard to see how

3. 'Sartre at Seventy: An Interview', *New York Review of Books*, August 1975.

the process could fail to cause great unhappiness, both to those losing protective secrecy and to those who would be hurt by the thoughts of others. Resistance would be so strong that there might develop an arms race of offensive and defensive technology: devices to jam the thought-reading machines, devices to jam the jammers, and so on. But if, after the horrors of the transition period, the world of the thought-reading machine became established, the effect on relationships might be much the same as that of voluntarily lowering the barriers. And it is not obvious that transparent relationships would be worse than opaque ones.

4 Identity and Individuality

In our present world, the sort of people we are is to some extent the result of our own choices. (The question of the extent to which our choices could have been different raises the problems about determinism and free will, which will not be discussed here. But, whatever the solution to those problems, most of us prefer to have our identity modifiable by our decisions.) It may be that privacy contributes to this control. Charles Fried has said that we often have thoughts we do not express, and that only when we choose to express them do we adopt them as part of ourselves. If the end of privacy is the end of any distinction between thoughts being endorsed and merely being entertained, then we may lose some control over our identity. It may have been some view of this kind which led Justices Warren and Brandeis to argue that a legal right to privacy is independent of more general property rights: 'The principle which protects personal writings and all other personal productions, not against theft and physical appropriation, but against publication in any form, is in reality not the principle of private property, but that of an inviolate personality.'[4]

In suggestions of this kind, there is something obscure about the idea of personality or identity. For what a person is depends on all his features, including those concealed from others. A sufficiently subtle thought-reading machine would detect the difference between thoughts merely coming to mind and thoughts being endorsed. All that would be lost is concealment of thoughts only entertained. But it is part of me that I do entertain those thoughts, and my identity is not changed because

4. 'The Right to Privacy', *Harvard Law Review* 1890.

this aspect of it comes to light. So when people say that transparency might threaten our freedom to choose our identity, they may not have in mind 'identity' in the sense of being a particular kind of person, but 'identity' in a sense closer to 'image of ourselves projected to other people'. It is obviously true that the abolition of privacy will reduce the control we have over the pictures other people have of us. But this seems more of a threat to our reputation than to our identity. Our freedom to define ourselves, when not just a matter of manipulation of image, is our freedom to choose between beliefs and attitudes, and to opt for some kinds of actions and ways of life rather than others. And this is not destroyed by others knowing what different ideas we have also considered.

Perhaps the threat posed by transparency is more oblique. It may be that public scrutiny of my mind does not in itself change my identity, but rather has effects which will inhibit the development of individuality. You will know when I am contemplating the ideas and actions you disapprove of, and I will know at once of your attitude. This may create very strong pressures to conform. John Stuart Mill wrote in 1859 of the social pressures towards respectability and conformity: 'In our times, from the highest class of society down to the lowest, everyone lives as under the eye of a hostile and dreaded censorship.'[5] One result of transparency might be to extend the social censorship inwards, so that there would be the same pressures for conformity of thought and feeling as there are for conformity of behaviour. We have only partial control over our thoughts and feelings, but the social censorship might persuade us to turn away from lines of thought which we knew might lead us into dangerous areas, as well as not to act on ideas arousing disapproval.

Privacy is necessary if we are not to be stifled by other people. Even in our present world, without the thought-reading machine, being permanently observed, as in some prisons, can destroy individuality. (Sartre, in an earlier phase, talked in *Being and Nothingness* with an almost neurotic horror of being observed by other people, and vividly presented the awfulness of permanent scrutiny in *Huis Clos*, where hell for three people is being locked for ever in a room together.) To be observed by other people can build up a feeling of pressure to justify what we are doing and how we are doing it, or to justify doing nothing. For many people, happiness, and perhaps creativity and originality, flourish where there are long stretches free from critical appraisal.

5. *On Liberty*, chapter 3

Perhaps we have the potential to grow more robust, and in a world of transparent relationships we might grow stronger in our resistance to pressures to conform. But it is hard to see how the extra pressures could be avoided, with their obvious threat to individuality.

5 The Two Perspectives

I have suggested that transparency would not in itself threaten our identity, and that its effects on relationships might, after a transition period, be beneficial. But it is plausible that it would allow new and powerful social pressures for conformity. If this account is accepted, our view of any proposed steps towards the transparent world will depend on how we weigh these different gains and losses. Any appraisal is difficult because it is hard to imagine relationships so transformed. If the threat to individuality seems much more clear than the benefits to relationships, many of us will be very cautious in our attitude to the dismantling of the barriers of privacy.

Yet it may be that our horror at the thought of entering the transparent world is nothing to the horror with which people in the transparent world will look back at our lives. They may think of us as hiding behind barriers of mutual pretence, like the inhabitants of a suburban street hiding behind fences and hedges. They might be far more concerned to avoid the reinstatement of the barriers of privacy than we are to avoid them being dismantled. The conflict between their perspective and ours, which will reappear in other contexts, raises a deep theoretical difficulty in deciding what sort of world we should aim for.

Chapter 5 Mood

'HAPPY' PILLS KEEP THE OUTPUT FLOWING

It could be the answer that Britain's troubled car industry has been seeking – a little white tablet that keeps production workers happy.

The Japanese motor industry believes it is an important aid to its productivity and now workers at a British car plant are being invited to take a daily dose of ginseng.

Doctors who are hoping to start clinical tests next month are anxious to cast aside ginseng's reputation as a Chinese aphrodisiac, claiming that its true effect is to reduce stress and act as a tonic.

'It is of the greatest help to people who are under pressure or who have monotonous jobs,' said Mr Hamilton Cooper, managing director of English Grains, manufacturing chemists of Burton-on-Trent, which is providing ginseng tablets for the test.

Volunteers on the production line and in the administrative offices will get daily ginseng tablets, the others fake tablets. Their feelings and job performance will then be compared with those of workers who have received nothing.

And the firm involved? 'Well, it's not British Leyland although I'm certain they will be keen to see the published results,' said Mr Cooper. 'At the moment the doctors who will be running the tests are talking to union representatives about the scheme. Results in other countries are impressive. Two of the big Japanese car makers give free ginseng to their workers and what's their productivity – about three times ours? And workers at the great new Lada car plant in Russia receive it.'

If the results of the proposed tests should interest British Leyland, supplying ginseng to the company's work force would cost about £4.5 million a year – the equivalent of half a day's lost production.

But what about those aphrodisiac rumours? 'We certainly make no claims about this,' said Mr Cooper. 'But it is common sense that if you feel good and are not shattered after a day's work then you are probably going to have a better sex life. It is significant that many car workers complain about this so I imagine the doctors will be interested in this aspect. The fact is that a happy person makes a better worker.'

GUARDIAN, 10 January 1980

The remarkable growth in the medical use of anti-depressant and other mood-changing drugs is well known. Psychochemicals have already made a great impact on people's lives, and many find the implications of this disturbing. The anxieties are partly about the power of manipulation that such drugs may confer. If governments, the police or employers were allowed unrestricted use of them, whole populations might become malleable to a degree never before possible. Those of us who do not want to be at the mercy of the authorities are right to watch the development of these drugs, and of social restrictions on their use, very carefully.

But concern about possible misuse of these chemicals by the authorities does not exhaust our anxiety. Many would still resist a society with widespread reliance on mood-changing drugs even with no exploitation for manipulative purposes. And the resistance does not depend simply on worries about the possibility of harmful side effects. There are various different objections, which are worth separating out.

1 The Objection to Social Quietism

If a man with a large family becomes unemployed, he may become sufficiently depressed to seek medical help. His doctor may put him on anti-depressant drugs. There is not much else the doctor on his own can do. His other patients leave him little time for transforming society, and the drug will probably relieve the depression. But when, in different cases, we see this decision repeated over and over again, we may start to ask questions. We may question the adequacy of leaving these problems in the 'medical' category, to be dealt with by doctors on an individual basis. Perhaps some people have such a strong genetic predisposition to depression that it would come whatever happened in their lives. But it seems likely that what happens to people plays an important part. An effective attack on depression might need social changes. We would probably have to change our economic priorities, taking seriously the eradication of unemployment and of family poverty. We might need to encourage people to take more control over their working lives, and to transform the nature of work. We might need to stop housing people in unsuitable buildings, and to create a less ugly environment. Perhaps most of all (and this would need deeper and more elusive changes than political ones) we would need to change the attitudes that cause neglect and loneliness.

These social changes are all hard to bring about, and take a long time. Where drugs can give immediate help, it is natural that they are used. But it is disturbing that they may be used, not just as first aid, but as a substitute for tackling the real problems. In a city or country hit by economic disaster, the political or social response may be for people to organize themselves to create work, to demand changes of policy or of government, and to plan how future disasters can be avoided. This contrasts favourably with an alternative response, where the members of a decaying community lose hope of reversing the disaster. and escape by using drugs to change their states of consciousness.

This political or social objection to the psychological approach to problems is clearly important. A central feature of the objection is that the social problems, being left unsolved, are left to trouble others. Despite its importance, this does not go to the deepest level of our resistance. For the objection could be met by leaving society as it is, and making mood-changing drugs available to all. That way, no one would be left distressed by the unsolved problems. Many of us have doubts which go beyond the objection that drugs only tackle problems on an individual basis.

2 Appropriateness

In the normal run of things, our moods are usually roughly appropriate to the things that happen to us. People are cheerful when about to go on holiday, depressed on failing examinations, irritable when stuck in a traffic jam. Our responses are no doubt also influenced by our chemical state. But in general we can give reasons for our moods that are intelligible to people with no knowledge of our chemistry. Moods are perhaps the most primitive part of our emotional life. As we go up the scale to more complex emotional states we find that their sophistication is bound up with more subtle distinctions between the circumstances to which they are appropriate responses. Grief is not just a free-floating mood in the way depression or anxiety can be, but is tied to bereavement or other loss. The difference between such states as embarrassment, shame and guilt is not a difference between introspectible sensations, but depends on social conventions and on our beliefs about what we have done.

The more complex emotional states involve beliefs, but also depend on the presence of some of the feelings and dispositions involved in the more primitive moods. In this way, mood-changing drugs can alter our more sophisticated emotions too. Suppose I hear the news of the death of someone close to me just after I have taken a dose of a very powerful drug for inducing a mood of cheerfulness. However many of the appropriate beliefs I have (about how awful it is, how there will be a gap that can never be filled), I cannot be said to be in a state of grief if my underlying mood is of irrepressible cheerfulness. My whole emotional state is inappropriate to what has happened.[1] And part of our resistance to the massive and widespread use of mood-changing drugs is their tendency to weaken the link between what happens to a person and his emotional response. At the extreme, emotional states become no more justifiable or unjustifiable than the weather is.

This is not to deny that our normal, appropriate, emotional states also depend on our chemistry. No doubt the things that make an emotional impact on us trigger off chemical changes. And if humans had a different set of neurochemical systems, our emotional responses might naturally be like those that would now result from some drug. So why are we disturbed at the thought of drugs changing our responses from those which, being standard, are now considered appropriate? Two reasons suggest themselves, one to do with membership of the human community, and the other to do with our sense of identity.

We do not always have the same responses to the same things. But sympathy, friendship and love depend on our emotional reactions only varying within a limited range. Like molecules made to hook on to each other, we can make psychological contact only because at least some of our responses fit together. (Think of someone, perhaps a Charles Addams character, irrepressibly cheerful at funerals, and highly amused at news of air crashes or kidnappings.)

1. There are links between complex emotions and more primitive moods, which are at least as responsive to our chemistry as to our beliefs. These links set severe limits to Spinoza's attractive programme of eliminating subjection to unwanted emotions by realizing the irrationality of the beliefs they are bound up with.

The importance of shared responses is a good reason for a single person being reluctant to embark on any drastic course of mood-changing. But this is not the whole story. If a whole community went on mood-changing drugs, everyone might be changed in the same way, with no resulting loss of sympathy and understanding. Yet we may still resist the change. Our emotional responses are too central to our sense of who we are for us willingly to accept sudden changes. If you tamper too drastically with my emotions, friendship may still be possible with people similarly altered, but it may be unclear to what extent it will be me who has the friends.

My sense of identity is at stake. The sort of person I am, the sort of emotions and attitudes I have, depend on such factors as my chemistry and my experiences. These may change over time, and after forty years I may be a very different person with a very different outlook. But, in the normal course of things, the changes will be gradual, and depend a lot on my decisions and on my interpretation of what happens to me. The gradualness allows me to see myself as a continuous person despite the changes. And the active role of my choices and outlook makes my life one of continuous self-creation, rather than just a sequence of passive changes of mood independent of my beliefs.

Suppose a man hears that the political party he supports has just lost an election. He may feel depressed for a bit, and this mood change is no doubt bound up with changes in his chemistry. The fact that his depression has a chemical basis is in no way undermining of his autonomy. For these chemical changes are dependent on the beliefs he has. If, before the election, reflection had led him to switch his support to the opposing party, his mood and chemical state would now be different.

On the other hand, some chemically based mood-changes are a threat to autonomy. The same man may work in a car factory. If the managers have decided that 'a happy person makes a better worker', and have, without his agreement, put mood-changing drugs in the water used for making tea, his emotional changes are independent of his own beliefs and outlook. Frequent changes in the drug used may produce a kaleidoscope of different emotional states which are in no way related to his underlying character. To that extent, his control over the sort of person he is has been undermined.

3 The Superdrug

We can imagine a drug programme which would not be vulnerable to any of the objections raised. Suppose a superdrug is developed for altering mood, which has no side-effects involving any risk or impairment to health, and which is in no way addictive. It does not lead to any blurring of awareness or to lethargy. Its effect, on the contrary, is to make people more alert and invigorated. Although it induces a good mood and a sense of well-being under normal conditions, its effect is not so overriding as to rule out different emotional responses where they are appropriate to the person's beliefs about what happens. It induces no tendency to social quietism.

Let us also suppose that the superdrug is never used to influence others' behaviour, but is only used by people to affect their own mood. Everyone in the community is fully informed about its effects, and it is only taken knowingly and voluntarily. (This last condition raises familiar problems. But assume that taking the drug involves some complicated procedure which will virtually never be gone through inadvertently. Also assume that no one puts any pressure on anyone else to take it, and that it is not available to children or to the mentally disturbed or subnormal.)

The superdrug is a test case of how deep someone's objections to mood-changing drugs go. I can see nothing wrong with it at all. I have already outlined my own sources of resistance, ranging from obvious surface objections to do with bad side-effects, to deeper concerns with identity and autonomy. The superdrug has been deliberately specified in a way that meets those objections.

Some people will have more stubborn resistance, and they will reject the superdrug. I am sure I have not thought of all conceivable objections. But one plausible source of further opposition has to do with the un-naturalness of altering psychological states by means of drugs, and is perhaps bound up with the thought that we ought to change the world to suit us as we are, rather than change ourselves to be more cheerful in the world as it is. In part this objection has been met by the stipulation that the superdrug does not induce quietism. But there is a residual objection about the unnaturalness of changing the sort of people we are, which will be discussed in more general terms in Chapter 12.

Although the superdrug is unobjectionable, its beneficial effects on our emotional life seem likely to be confined to a single dimension. Mood is at the primitive end of our emotional life. We are cheerful or depressed, relaxed or anxious, calm or irritable, and these moods matter to us and to people we live with. But it is a feature of moods that, while they can be triggered off by particular experiences or thoughts, they are often rather diffuse and poorly focused. Within this dimension, the superdrug could be very valuable. It is better to feel cheerful or exhilarated than to feel anxious, depressed or irritable, and because of this, many of us would take the drug. And if large doses of it would give us ecstatic feelings of well-being, or a deep, 'mystical' feeling of being in harmony with the universe, we might feel greatly enriched by such experiences.

But, however intense the experiences it gave, a drug limited to these general effects on our diffusely focused moods would have only oblique effects on what is perhaps a more interesting dimension of our emotional life. Mood, compared to the more complex parts of our emotional life, is relatively independent of relationships and beliefs. The contrast here is with the process by which primitive emotions become more diverse and subtle as people have new and shared experiences, talk to each other, and learn to see and think about things in new ways. In a single person's life, simple feelings of early childhood, like anger and fear, liking and hostility, may develop into an emotional life of Proustian gradation and subtlety. And, although we have to be very cautious in our interpretation here, it is perhaps possible to see the outlines of a similar process in the history of the human race. The reasons for caution are obvious. We have in general only the evidence of letter-writers, poets, novelists and painters about the emotional life of people at other times. It is hard to separate limitations of experience from limitations in the skill of a writer or painter, or from limitations in what has been selected for portrayal. And a crude belief in emotional 'progress' will make us think that we are more perceptive about people than Rembrandt or Tolstoy. It is also true that a more ramified and subtle consciousness may involve losses as well as gains. Peasants and primitive tribesmen may have a directness and warmth lost to many readers of Proust. But, when all these warnings are kept in mind, it is hard not to see at least a fitful development in the direction of wider sympathies and more subtly discriminated states of consciousness.

As with scientific progress, what is gained at one time can be lost again. And, just as many people alive now have far less grasp of science than Newton had, so we have emotional primitives among us now. But perhaps there is also, as with science, a kind of progress, so that some of Proust's readers have a more developed consciousness than any of Chaucer's contemporary audience.

Many readers will be out of sympathy with the historical speculations vaguely gestured at in the last two paragraphs. Perhaps they are right to be sceptical. But, even if changes in relationships and emotional life do not come near the progress we have made in our intellectual understanding of the world, it still seems that many of the most interesting emotional developments come because people live differently, and because they see things differently. The things we do together, and talk to each other about, change the less primitive parts of our emotional life. Drugs operating only on diffuse moods may give us certain kinds of intense and valuable experience. But, if they are to bring radical changes along other dimensions, they will have to affect our beliefs and our way of seeing things.

Other objections to mood-changing drugs apply more generally to all techniques for influencing and controlling people.

Chapter 6 Control

A certain fascination and fear associated with observing and possibly controlling behaviour at a distance still exists among a substantial number of psychologists as well as the general public. If such techniques of instrumentation are to become more than experimental curiosities or science-fiction nightmares. we are obliged to seek ways of building into our apparatus more precision, flexibility and aesthetic appeal.

Robert L. Schwitzgebel and Richard M. Bird: *Sociotechnical Design Factors in Remote Instrumentation with Humans in Natural Environments*

Supposing it were possible to get houses built, corn grown, battles fought, causes tried, and even churches erected and prayers said, by machinery – by automatons in human form – it would be a considerable loss to exchange for these automatons even the men and women who at present inhabit the more civilized parts of the world, and who assuredly are but starved specimens of what nature can and will produce. Human nature is not a machine to be built after a model, and set to do exactly the work prescribed for it, but a tree, which requires to grow and develop itself on all sides, according to the tendency of the inward forces which make it a living thing.

John Stuart Mill: *On Liberty*

Human actions are the product of desires, beliefs and abilities. People wanting to control the actions of others have always had techniques for operating on all three. Incentives or threats either create new desires or strengthen existing ones. Beliefs can be changed by spreading information, or by propaganda and advertising. A person's ability to perform some action may be impaired or eliminated by taking away his money or by sending him to prison. Much political conflict has been over the permissibility of these different kinds of influence, and over who should have control of these techniques of persuasion, and when. It is not surprising that the prospect of psychology and neurobiology providing new kinds of behaviour control is seen as potentially dangerous.

The new techniques which are seen as most threatening operate by means of influencing desires and abilities, and not, at least primarily, by influencing beliefs. It is true that hallucinogenic drugs or subliminal persuasion are new ways of altering people's beliefs, but their applications seem fairly limited. The psychological methods which suggest the most disturbing prospects of control are various kinds of conditioning and behaviour therapy – the techniques arising from neurobiology and drugs which influence moods and desires, electrical stimulation of the brain, and psychosurgery. All these methods are now being developed, and each of them seems to offer the prospect of controlling people by means of altering their desires more directly than has been possible before.

The psychological techniques involve encouraging some kinds of behaviour by reward, and discouraging other kinds by associating them with something unpleasant, such as an electric shock, or being made to vomit. (The vomiting technique is vividly described by Anthony Burgess in *A Clockwork Orange*, where Alex is cured of his aggression by this association.) Behaviour therapy has varying success, but when it works it does so either by eliminating a desire (to fight, say, or to smoke), or by generating or strengthening a countervailing desire.

The neurobiological techniques all involve direct physical or chemical action on the brain. As well as drugs altering moods and desires, brain surgery can bring about irreversible psychological changes. But perhaps the most dramatic demonstrations of power to control behaviour come from electrical stimulation of the brain. One well known case is that of an aggressive bull, in whose brain José Delgado implanted electrodes. When it was in full charge, it could be stopped by a radio signal stimulating its brain. Delgado says, 'the result seemed to be a combination of motor effect, forcing the bull to stop and to turn to one side, plus behavioural inhibition of the aggressive drive.'[1] Delgado's interpretation of his study has been disputed, on the grounds that the interference with the control of movement was enough to stop the bull, so that there may have been no direct reduction of aggressive desire. It may be that, despite the reactions of alarm to such publicized cases, we are not yet at the stage of being able

1. José M. R. Delgado: *Physical Control of the Mind, Toward a Psychocivilized Society*, New York, 1969, p. 168. Delgado's account is criticized in Elliot S. Valenstein: *Brain Control*, New York, 1973, pp. 98–104.

to switch desires on and off by electrical stimulation. And it *may* turn out that the brain works in such a way as to present insuperable obstacles in principle to any such project. But those of us who are alarmed by some of the possible uses of such techniques have as yet no basis for the comfortable assumption that such insuperable barriers must exist. Remote-control brain-stimulation is moving on from the crude use of an electrical stimulus to the more subtle technique of releasing chemicals. We have hardly begun to explore the different effects that different chemicals have when released at different sites in the brain. We are in no position to claim that these techniques will never lead to desires being switched on and off by remote control. So it is worth asking questions now about what sort of use, if any, we ought to make of such techniques.

1 Some Questions

Conditioning techniques, certain drugs, and perhaps some kinds of brain stimulation, all alter behaviour by altering desires. Because of this, they are alarming and controversial. But all sorts of uncontroversial activities also alter people's behaviour by altering their desires. To marry someone, to employ someone, to send someone to school, are all likely to generate in them new desires. Why are brain stimulation and behaviour therapy more disturbing than marriage and education? Is it because the new techniques are more powerful? Or is it that they are open to new and different kinds of abuse? Or is it that there is something about them which is objectionable in principle, independent of particular ways in which they could be abused?

Some methods of influencing people are more objectionable than others. Persuasion by offering a reward or other positive inducement is better than coercion by threat. A rational person would not choose to have his options altered by someone else's threats, but he might choose to have them altered by some positive inducement. Aversion therapy of the kind used to cure Alex's aggression can be seen as a kind of coercion: 'Be good or feel sick.' In this way it is worse than conditioning by means of reward.[2]

2. These points come from Robert Nozick: 'Coercion', in S. Morgenbesser *et al.* (eds.), *Philosophy, Science and Method: Essays in Honor of Ernest Nagel*, New York, 1969, and P. S. Greenspan: 'Behavior Control and Freedom of Action,' *Philosophical Review* 1978.

Other differences in our response to different methods have a less clear basis. Although many widely used drugs have drastic effects on behaviour, there is a greater sense of horror at the thought of people being manipulated by brain stimulation. In part, this may be because drugs have to be re-administered, which gives the person some opportunity to resist or escape, while the implanted electrode can be stimulated almost regardless of the person's activity. But it is hard to believe that this fully explains the different responses we have, although it is not clear what further reason there could be. It would be bizarre to object specifically to electricity, so that brain stimulation would be acceptable when electrodes were replaced by chemi-trodes. An alternative would be to distinguish between unacceptably applying chemicals directly to the brain, and acceptably doing so indirectly by an orally administered drug. There seem no plausible reasons to support this position.

The aim of this chapter is to separate out some of the different reasons for objecting to present or possible future technology of behaviour control. The objections come at different levels, like the layers of an onion. The outer layers are the most important now and in the near future. They concern the relatively immediate and very serious dangers of unscrupulous misuse. The inner layers are objections even to the benevolent use of these techniques. In the world as it is, they are less urgent, but they raise the deeper philosophical questions.

2 Abuse by the Authorities

One obvious reason for fearing the development of behaviour control is the near certainty that governments will abuse it to make people obey them. To take just two examples: we know how psychiatric drugs have been used in Russia, and we know how knowledge of the effects of sensory deprivation has been applied in Northern Ireland. But there is a case for saying we have nothing further to fear from the invention of more methods of the same kind. For these are crude techniques, which manipulate their victims by inflicting horrors on them, and manipulate other people by fear. The available array of tortures and horrors is so great that adding to it may not increase the world's misery. A victim may be relatively indifferent between newer sensory deprivation and old-fashioned electric shocks.

It is the development of more subtle techniques which might enlarge the powers of evil governments. From the point of view of these governments, rule by fear and torture must be a messy affair, generating problems of its own. It would be much simpler if techniques existed to make people want to behave in the desired way. For this reason, the development of effective and painless ways of moulding desires will raise the danger of ruling groups vastly extending their power over populations. There is the consoling thought that some techniques (such as those involving the implanting of electrodes in the brain) could only be applied to people virtually enslaved already. But this reassurance may not apply to all techniques developed for manipulatory desires. Where it does not, the possibility of governmental abuse raises doubts whether research on such techniques could be justifiable.

3 Benevolent Control by the Authorities

The drawbacks of behaviour control in the hands of an ill-intentioned government are obvious. The drawbacks of it in the hands of a benevolent government are less obvious, and are not the immediate problem. But the more subtle anxieties start to emerge only when we consider the benevolent use of techniques of control.

We can conceive of the authorities, in the distant future, deciding to eliminate conflict, and to increase happiness, by controlling the desires people have. (Imagine a technique for stimulation of particular sites in the brain without any apparatus being implanted there.) The temptation to damp down or eliminate desires which lead to violent crime is clear. So is the temptation to eliminate the desire not to live next door to people of another race. It would soon be seen how many problems and conflicts could be solved by changing people's desires, and an enthusiastically benevolent government could find itself becoming in this respect increasingly interventionist. This thought is horrifying to most of us, despite the prospect that a community manipulated in this way might be without the major social sources of unhappiness. Why is the prospect so disturbing?

The first objections involve doubts about whether we really would find the resulting world an improvement. Can we rely on the effectiveness of the controllers in making us happier? So many well-intentioned social plans depend on predictions that turn out to be mistaken, that it is hard to feel optimistic about handing such power to a government. There is also the anxiety about whether we could trust in the controllers' continued benevolence. To know that they have the power to give us self-destructive desires is to doubt whether any evidence about their present good intentions would be sufficiently reassuring about the future. And handing over this power would be irreversible unless the controllers decided otherwise. They could switch off any desires we later had to re-assert our own control.

Other objections could be made from our present standpoint, independent of whether life under a system of behaviour control would seem satisfying at the time. Social harmony might be purchased at a great cost in regimentation and uniformity. We now value having a huge variety of different kinds of people with very varied patterns of life. The prospective loss of this may now seem a serious drawback, despite the fact that no regrets may be felt later because the preference for variety could be eliminated.

Another objection concerns equality. Why should *they* control *us*? In our present world we can dislike someone being in a position to make us do things, even if what we are made to do is only what we would have done in any case. If we dislike inequalities of power, this is another drawback, even if our preferences are later going to be manipulated so that we will no longer object.

These objections to the benevolent use of behaviour control are perhaps enough to show that any scheme likely to be devised would *at least* have to have formidable countervailing advantages to stand any chance of being acceptable to those of us who hold them. But there are objections at a deeper level, which can be brought out by imagining a system designed to meet those raised so far.

4 Voluntary Submission to Democratically Programmed Control

Suppose the members of a community are considering a 'democratic' version of behaviour control. The idea is that their desires will be monitored, and sometimes altered, by a machine. But this machine will itself be programmed in advance by the members of the community. The machine will have fed into it a huge amount of information about the psychology of each person, so that it knows more about them all than any one of them does. And the instructions they give it are to alter their desires where this will lead to greater happiness.

The alterations to desires could take several forms. Some would only involve matters internal to a single person. The person wanting to be a painter, but who would be much more successful as an engineer, would have his desires changed accordingly. (Assume that, while the machine can alter desires, it cannot alter abilities.) Other changes would be in people's relationships. The machine would ensure that love was always mutual, and that parents' wishes for their children always harmonized with children's wishes for themselves. And, if technology had not eliminated all unpleasant jobs, they would start to seem pleasant to people given the right desires. Those now bored by accountancy would start to find it as interesting as some find stamp collecting.

A system of this kind could be guided by various different principles, according to the outlook of those setting it up. The aim could be the greatest total happiness, regardless of whether some people are much happier than others. Or, questions of distribution could also be brought in. The aim might be equality of happiness, or else some arrangement where no one fell below a certain level. Whatever system was chosen, a lot of present misery and frustration would be eliminated. Conflict would be replaced by harmony, both within each person and between people. It is likely that everyone would feel some benefit.

If a lot of communities opted for behaviour control of this kind, we might start to compare the kinds of life they had with those of other societies. No doubt cross-cultural comparisons pose many problems, but we might get some idea of the strengths and weaknesses of the two patterns of life. The difficulties might be of the same order as comparing the success in India of western-style marriages and of those arranged by parents in the traditional way. It is hard to imagine how a programmed society would strike us. But the elimination of conflict and frustration are large gains which might not easily be outweighed.

This democratic system of behaviour control would bring these benefits without being open to the objections against versions where some people control others. There would be no inequality of power. No one would be at the mercy of anyone else's changes of outlook. If the machine was given enough knowledge of people's psychology, its plans would not turn out wrongly. And sufficiently many fail-safe devices would remove anxieties about the machine itself going wrong. If the people setting up the system disliked regimentation and uniformity, they could draw up a programme to favour the widest variety of desires and ways of life. And, above all, it would be voluntary. There would obviously be problems where a majority wanted the system and a minority did not. But suppose it is only adopted where it has unanimous support.

Perhaps the democratic version can be designed in a way which meets the previous layer of objections to behaviour control. Yet a great deal of resistance remains. We can recognize that we might all be much happier in such a society, and yet still feel that, from our present standpoint, there is something repugnant about the scheme. We have another layer of objections.

5 A Closed Society

One source of our reluctance may be the value we place on keeping open the possibility of change. We do not want to rule out fundamental change in human life, or in our ways of seeing it. The changes of belief and outlook in the history even of a single culture make us see the future as unpredictable and open. Some of the pleasure of being human is to be part of this open-ended development of our species. The unpredictable unfolding of human consciousness can seem the most remarkable process we know.

An anxiety about a community submitting to behaviour control, even of the most benevolent or democratic kind, is that this might end the further development of consciousness. New kinds of life, and new ways of seeing things, may depend on allowing free play to desires which, at least at first, are socially disruptive. A benevolent machine, lacking an omniscient grasp of all possible future ways of thought, would probably play safe, and damp down desires and attitudes of disruptive originality. In handing ourselves over to it, we might be opting to stay forever within the limitations of our present outlook. At the most fundamental level, life and thought might become static.

It may be thought that we could programme the machine to favour fundamental changes of outlook. But it is then not clear how far this would differ from ordinary life, or, even worse, how far it differs from handing over to a machine that we have not programmed at all.

6 Identity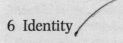

The desires we have are a central part of our picture of who we are. This is why behaviour control, even of the most benevolent kind, can threaten our identity. If I am told that I will be happier after a radical transformation of my desires and outlook, I may wonder to what extent the happier person will be *me*. The new desires may be ones that I now would disapprove of. Or they may be so different from any I have now that the main plans and projects of my life are changed unrecognizably.

This is not to say that all our present desires are important to our sense of identity. Some are too trivial to matter. And others, although they play an important role in my life, may be ones I do not identify with. People who seek behaviour therapy to rid themselves of their addiction to smoking or their deviant sexual tastes are indicating that they do not identify with these desires, and would prefer to be without them. But for most of us there is a central core of desires and attitudes with which we identify. In this central region, these desires and attitudes to a great extent determine our picture of ourselves, and any attempt by other people to bring about substantial changes here would be seen as a threat to our identity.

It may be objected that this makes our identity a more rigid matter than it usually is. Our desires and attitudes can conflict with each other and, more importantly, they often change over time. The facets of my outlook that I now look on as part of the central core may seem much less important in ten years' time, and in twenty years may all have been abandoned.

But the fact that the central core changes does not make its defence less important to our identity. We know our desires and outlook may be very different in twenty or thirty years, but it matters to us that this should come about by a gradual evolution of a relatively self-directed kind. In part, the changes will result from external factors: if I go and live in Canada, this will alter the way my outlook evolves. But it matters that the resulting outlook will come from *my* responses to Canada, and

87

also that the decision to go or stay is mine. Living our own lives involves being able, at least in part, to mould ourselves. It would be an absurd exaggeration to say that we can be any type of person we choose. Our desires do not have such power over our nature. But it would be equally wrong to deny that our present decisions have an important influence on the sort of people we will be in future. Although we rarely think of it except when it is threatened, this project of continuous self-creation is a central one in our lives. This is what we give up when we hand over to others, or to a machine, the power to wipe out our present desires and to create new ones.

7 Self-Modification

Suppose people were given the ability to switch on and off their own desires, by electrical or chemical stimulation of particular sites in their brains. One danger would be of other people taking control of the stimulating equipment, and so gaining overwhelming power over them. But if, for theoretical purposes, we ignore this possibility, or imagine it somehow guarded against, would giving us this power of self-modification be a good thing?

It is hard to be sure what the impact on our life would be. One possibility is that people's emotional lives would become trivial and shallow. Another is that people would have a stronger sense of being self-directed, and find it easier to realize their deeper commitments. Everything would depend on the extent to which the person had developed a stable outlook, with a relatively permanent central core of desires strong enough to dominate the decisions about the use of the self-modifying techniques.

Using brain stimulation to switch desires on and off would itself always be determined by other desires. A person who wants to be healthy or lose weight might switch on a desire to take some exercise, or switch off a desire to eat. A man who wants to be faithful to his wife might switch off a desire for another woman. In these cases the desires representing stable, long-term commitments and projects dominate the decision, and switch off temporary desires which, at a deeper level, we do not identify with. But the alternative is also possible. The person who wants to be lazy or to eat might switch off his desire to lose weight, so that his enjoyment would be undisturbed by guilt or self-criticism. The man who wants another woman might switch off his desire to be faithful to his wife.

The outcome depends on whether the central desires the person identifies with are stronger than the immediate and distracting ones at the time of the decision. In this way, our position with the new technology would resemble the present. For, whether or not I eat more than I should depends in our present world on whether my immediate desire to eat is stronger at the moment of decision than my longer-term desire to lose weight. The technique of brain stimulation would just give us the power to eliminate whichever desire loses the contest. (It may also be easier to switch off a desire than to continue resisting it over time.)

In our present-day life, there are two extreme possibilities. There is the person whose central projects effectively dominate his life, and who succeeds in regulating all other desires, so that they fail to divert him from the activities he has decided to be most important. At the other extreme is the person whose actions are always dominated by immediate impulses, and who has either no long-term commitments or else only ineffective ones. Most of us are at points on a continuum between these extremes, being relatively strong-willed about some things and quite a bit at the mercy of immediate impulses about others. Having the ability to switch off desires that lose the contest seems likely to make us more sharply different from each other. The strong-willed person will be even less influenced by distracting desires, as they will be eliminated. The impulsive person will become even more so, as he will eliminate the longer-term desires when they threaten to impair his immediate pleasure.

The implications of self-modification would in this way vary for different people. But for those with a reasonably coherent dominant outlook, the new techniques would help rather than hinder self-creation across a lifetime. For such people, this would count in favour of these new powers over their desires.

8 Conclusions

The greatest and the nearest threats from new techniques for controlling desires and behaviour are that some groups of people, perhaps govern-ments, will gain further power over others, and put this power to bad ends. Few of us need reminding of this. Many of us are also alarmed by the benevolent use of behaviour control. Our objections have partly to do with the danger of the controllers making mistakes, and with the irreversibility of their power over us, and partly to do with the inequality between controllers and controlled. We also fear an imposed uniformity. But there is a deeper objection which remains when these first ones have been met. Whatever the quality of the world in which we are controlled, we are reluctant to purchase it at the cost of no longer directing our own lives, and no longer choosing what sort of people to be. When techniques of self-manipulation are given to us, our project of self-creation may survive or even be helped. When the techniques of manipulation pass to others, this central feature of our lives is lost.

None of this is to say that manipulating other people is never justifiable. At present, for important social purposes, we try to influence people's desires and behaviour by crude and only partly effective techniques, such as the threat of prison. And it may be that sufficiently large social gains could justify the use of more intrusive techniques. (One person having the ability to switch off another's aggression might give great protection to many who are now victims of acts of violence.) But any proposed extension of behaviour control has to be assessed, not only in terms of whatever immediate advantage it offers, but also in the context of the sort of world we will end up with if each piecemeal extension is allowed.

Chapter 7 Dreams (I)

'Yes, I heard voices down along the river somewhere – a man's voice and a woman's voice calling.'

When she was asked how she could tell the calling had been 'along the river', she said, 'I don't know. It seems to be one I was visiting when I was a child.'

Warning without stimulation – 'Nothing.'

Three minutes later, without any warning, stimulation was carried out again probably near 13. While the electrode was held in place, she exclaimed 'Yes, I hear voices. It is late at night, around the carnival somewhere – some sort of travelling circus.' Then, after removal of the electrode: 'I just saw lots of big waggons that they use to haul animals in.'

Wilder Penfield: *The Excitable Cortex in Conscious Man*

In lucid dreams, conscious insight emerges within the dream state. It is like being awake, having 'freewill' and possessing 'critical faculties', but being in a totally artificial 'other' world, and at the same time knowing so . . . The period of lucidity may extend to several minutes, during which the dreamer observes his dream environment as he realizes that every intricate detail of the scene is purely an internal construction of the brain. Objects and people appear to be, and feel, solid and the lucid dreamer is able to converse with the dream characters. The quality of the visual imagery is sometimes reported to be even more detailed and vivid than in waking life. All the senses through which we perceive the world may be involved – such that the dreamer can, for example, taste and smell a wine . . .

I have devised a portable 'dream machine' . . . which detects REM sleep and automatically gives electrical impulses so as to 'trigger' lucidity. Several subjects have successfully undergone 'lucid dream induction' in the laboratory.

Keith Hearne: 'Control Your Own Dreams', *New Scientist*, 24 September 1981

Where drugs that change moods or desires also blur or reduce our awareness of things, this is an additional objection to them. We value seeing things as they are, free from distortions of consciousness. Because we value clear-headed awareness, we are uneasy if the price of contentment is diminished contact with reality. This objection to some kinds of psychological technology is a deep one, which is often obscured by other more visible dangers of altering mood and behaviour. The value placed on contact with reality is also less simple than it seems at first. My aim here is to make it clearer, and to raise some questions about it. The strategy will be to take an extreme case, repugnant to many of us, of exchanging reality for contentment. By asking what changes, if any, would make it acceptable, it may be possible to bring out in more detail what we value.

1 The Experience Machine

The extreme case is one of a machine developed to stimulate the brain in such a way that the person has a sequence of enjoyable experiences.[1] These bear no more relation to the external world (apart from the machine's programme) than dreams do. But the experiences would be an improvement on most dreams in that they would be indistinguishable from the equivalent real life experiences. Subjectively, the only difference from real life would be that a different set of experiences would be had: there might be more experiences of swimming or of making scientific discoveries, and no experiences of going to the dentist or of being dismissed from a job. The reality behind these experiences might be, as Robert Nozick suggests, that all the time you are floating in a tank with electrodes attached to your brain.

Some of us would be prepared to try the experience machine for brief periods. As an entertainment, it might be like an improved version of the cinema. It could also be a preferred alternative to anaesthetic, for those periods where we now choose to opt out of reality, such as during a painful operation. But most of us would not choose to be plugged

1. This idea has been discussed from time to time by philosophers, usually in the context of such machines being a possible objection to utilitarianism. One of the most interesting recent discussions is by Robert Nozick: *Anarchy, State and Utopia*, pp. 42–5. I borrow the term 'experience machine' from him.

into the machine for the rest of our lives, and would be appalled at any suggestion that we should be compulsorily plugged in. Yet the intensity of our resistance seems to need explaining. Is not pleasurable experience a lot of what we seek in life? Some people think this is all we ever seek. Even if this is an exaggeration, there surely have to be some strong reasons for turning down a lifetime of pleasurable experience. What are they?

2 Some Primitive Objections

The primitive objections to the experience machine are those which suggest that it would not even be satisfying from the subjective point of view. In the first place, we have great psychological resistance to the idea that the machine's reproduction of experiences would be perfect. When we try to imagine being on the machine, we find it hard not to imagine some loss of quality, so that things are fainter, or the colour is not quite right. Then we also think, as some of us do about the traditional picture of heaven, that a life designed to provide perpetual bliss would become very boring. But neither of these sources of resistance is theoretically interesting. Each can be dealt with by stipulating certain features of the machine. The reproduction of experiences is stipulated to involve no loss of quality. The experiences have the ideal amount of variety to suit each person. And, if pure pleasure becomes cloying, the programme will include just the right amount of misery and discomfort to add the required savour to the other experiences. The experience of success will only come after the experience of a bit of failure. The experience of a hot bath will sometimes be preceded by the experience of being cold and wet. But life on the machine will still differ subjectively from real life. In ordinary life there is for most people a surplus of distress, frustration and failure, over and above that required to flavour the rest of experience. The primitive objections miss the point, as our resistance remains even when the machine is modified to meet them.

The same holds for certain practical objections to the experience machine, such as whether it would break down, or how it would be maintained, or how costly in energy it would be. No doubt there would be many such problems. Forget them, or assume them overcome. (The experience machine is a thought experiment, not an election manifesto.) The point is that even without worrying over the practical problems, and even when the experiences would be subjectively very satisfying, we still object to a lifetime on the machine.

3 Internal and External Perspectives

When we are thinking about a kind of life, and trying to evaluate it, we can adopt an internal or an external perspective.

An internal perspective involves seeing things from the point of view of the person concerned. Consider a couple whose whole life centred on bringing up their children, and who both died just as the children were reaching adult life. Suppose, two years after their death, all the children are killed in an air crash. We may think it a mercy they did not live to see this. If we say that the air crash came too late to make the couple's lives less good, we are adopting the internal perspective. On this view, what matters is how they saw things, and a disaster to their project does not wreck their lives if it happens when they are past knowing about it. From an internal perspective, a life like that of Cézanne or Frege, ending in death without recognition, is in that way a tragedy.

To adopt an external perspective is to allow in considerations other than how things seem to the person involved. These other considerations may be information not available to the person, but available to us. We know the children were killed in the air crash. We know about the posthumous recognition of Cézanne and Frege. Or, there may be no difference in the information available from the two perspectives, but a difference in attitude, as between an enthusiastic jockey and someone who loathes horse racing. There are as many different external perspectives as there are differences of information or attitude.

If we think that how a kind of life seems from the internal perspective is all that matters about it, we will find the experience machine a fairly cheering prospect. But most of us do not take that view. The life of an extremely cheerful mental defective is not one we would choose, however satisfactory from the internal perspective. Nor would most of us choose a lifetime on the experience machine. Why not?

4 Other People

To most of us an essential ingredient of a happy or worthwhile life is contact with other people. On the experience machine we inhabit a private world, and never again make contact with others. This is enough to rule it out. It may be said that we will think we are meeting other people and having relationships with them. This may be enough to make the experience machine subjectively satisfying, but from our external perspective, it is still appalling, because our desire is to *have* relationships, not to think we are having them.

Another point important from our external perspective is that one person going on the experience machine may be bad for others. Suppose a man with a boring and badly paid job decides to spend the rest of his life on the machine, having the experiences of a rich and successful film producer. The effect on his family is likely to be disastrous. They lose his company, and they lose even the low income he brought in. (His wife will not get the social security benefits given to widows, and may have problems over getting his unemployment pay.) Such considerations would put many people off the project.

There are two theories, psychological hedonism and psychological egoism, which would make us surprised that concern for other people's interests would put someone off the experience machine. Psychological hedonism says that people are only motivated by pursuit of their own pleasure. The experience machine would be everyone's utopia if this were so. Psychological egoism says that we are only motivated by our own interests. This is a broader theory than hedonism, as it allows that we can have interests other than pleasure, but it too rules out altruism. If you hold this view, you will think people will never be put off the experience machine because others need them. If you think, as I do, that many would be put off, you have to reject psychological egoism. The experience machine does not satisfy our desires for others, but only makes us *think* they are satisfied.

5 Activity

We prefer active lives to passive ones. Life imprisonment in a cinema seat is not an agreeable thought, even for the more sedentary of us.

We like to be physically active partly because of the pleasurable sensations and other experiences involved, and these could be duplicated on the machine. We like to be active because it keeps us healthy, and this too could be taken care of. Our preference for activity goes deeper than these benefits of physical exercise. What is terrible about a lifetime in the cinema is not just the lack of exercise, but that we become merely passive consumers. We would take no more decisions, and never put any decisions into effect. It matters to us that we are in control of what we do. It matters to us that what we do makes a difference to the world, and that it stretches us. These things would all be absent from life on the experience machine. We would *think* we were active, and that what we did made a contribution, and was quite hard. But really, we would be passive consumers of the machine's programme.

Our concern to be active is not always just a concern with the results of that activity. A scientist who fails to solve a problem may not be quite consoled by hearing that someone else has succeeded. This is brought out by Robert Nozick, who sees the importance of activity as an objection to the experience machine. He points out that we would not think our objection met by the addition of a result machine, 'which produces in the world any result you would produce and injects your vector into any joint activity'.[2] Our concern that *we* should make a difference is not just a desire that a difference should be made.

6 Identity Objections

As with the abolition of privacy, and control of behaviour and mood, one of our concerns about the experience machine is its threat to our identity. As Nozick puts it, 'Someone floating in a tank is an indeterminate blob. There is no answer to the question of what a person is like who has long been in the tank. Is he courageous, kind, intelligent, witty, loving? It's not merely that it's difficult to tell; there's no way he is. Plugging into the machine is a kind of suicide.'[3]

This identity objection is really a cluster of different ones. There are four quite separate reasons that could be given for thinking of going on the machine as a kind of suicide. The first, and most radical, would

2. Nozick: *Anarchy, State and Utopia*, p. 44.
3. ibid., p. 43.

be that life on the machine would not be that of a person at all. The second is that, while there will be a person on the machine, he will not be me. The third has to do with my desire to have certain characteristics, such as being courageous, kind, intelligent, witty or loving. And the fourth has to do with the desire, discussed in the previous two chapters, for my characteristics to be at least partly dependent on my own decisions and choices.

7 The Kantian Objection

The first line of thought is that a lifetime on the machine is not compatible with being a person at all. The suggestion, ultimately derived from Kant,[4] is that the existence of a person involves more than just the occurrence of a series of experiences. It also involves some self-consciousness: some idea that the stream of experiences is not merely happening, but belongs to you. And for this, the argument goes, you need to be aware of the contrast between yourself and the rest of the world. Walking across Bodmin Moor, you do not interpret your experiences as an impersonal awareness of a series of changes in a fluid world. You recognize that the moor is something stable, existing independently of you. You know that there are many other angles from which it can be seen, but that you see it from your own changing point of view.

The objection is that it would not be possible for someone who spent all his life on the experience machine to form this concept of himself. For the machine gives us no contact with any world independent of our

4. Kant: *Critique of Pure Reason*, 'Transcendental Analytic', chapter 2. I have drawn on the discussion of Kant's argument in P. F. Strawson: *The Bounds of Sense*, London, 1966, pp. 97–112. In the 'Kantian objection' presented here, no attempt is made to separate the contributions of Kant and Strawson. I do not know how far either of them would think the objection applies to the experience machine as described. Strawson in particular argues only against the view that 'a possible experience, the contents of a consciousness, could theoretically consist of a succession of intrinsically disconnected sensory data somehow linked by memory and expectation' (p. 103). It is not clear that he would regard the experiences on the machine as 'intrinsically disconnected'.

I have not here been able to pursue the interesting issues raised by the later stages of the argument. There the suggestion is that, if I cannot ascribe experiences to myself, there will be no distinction between what is experienced and my recognition of it, and, without this, nothing can even rate as an experience.

own experiences. So we will not be able to make the necessary contrast between changes in our experiences and changes in the world. As a result, we will be unaware of any frontier between ourselves and the world, and so unaware of ourselves as having a distinct existence. Perhaps those who had formed the idea of themselves in the ordinary world might retain it after the transition to the machine. But the suggestion is that the experiences the machine provides would not alone be enough to generate such an idea. And, if we accept this, we may start to worry about whether a long time spent on the machine will erode the distinction, that we have built up in our present state, between ourselves and the world.

The heart of the Kantian objection is the way it applies to the extreme case, where someone is on the machine from birth. Is it really true that he would never be able to form a conception of himself, distinct from what he experiences? It is tempting to say that the suggestion is absurd, as we can so easily imagine spending time on the machine, and we can imagine retaining our sense of identity just as much as we do in the cinema. But this objection is too brisk. As Strawson points out, it is not enough to show what *we*, with our history, can imagine. Nothing follows about what the person permanently on the machine can conceptualize.

But even if this extrapolation from our own conceptions is too quick, there may still be something wrong with the Kantian suggestion. For the person on the machine has exactly the same subjective experiences that he would have had if he had grown up in part of the ordinary world that had the features selected by the machine's programmer. And, if this sequence of subjective experiences would have been enough in the ordinary world to generate the distinction between himself and the world, why should the same distinction not be generated by the same experiences when produced by the machine? It is true that, when a sheep runs across my path in the Bodmin Moor of the experience machine, my experience is not caused by the activity of any sheep that really exists. But I do not know this, and so it might be expected that I should build up all the beliefs and concepts that I would build up on the basis of similar experiences in the ordinary world.[5] Perhaps most of my beliefs would be false, but I might still acquire concepts and draw distinctions on the basis of them.

The view that someone brought up entirely on the machine would

5. For a different view, see Hilary Putnam: *Reason, Truth and History*, Cambridge, 1982, chapter 1.

never develop the distinction between himself and what he experiences is unproved, and does not have much plausibility. And, if that anxiety is not a serious one, we need hardly worry about the effects plugging into the machine would have on those of us who have already developed a robust sense of our identity.

8 Will It Still Be Me?

The second identity objection is the fear that the person on the machine will not be me. It is this that makes plugging into the machine seem a kind of suicide. But this objection suffers from the obscurity of the idea of personal identity. In an ordinary lifetime, people can change drastically, but we do not normally have worries about whether they are still the same person. Outside philosophical discussions, these worries only arise in rather extreme cases, such as loss of memory, and no doubt they will arise if surgeons start to offer us brain transplants. Philosophers have tried to make us articulate our concept of personal identity more clearly by presenting us with a wide range of imaginary cases, involving people making amoeba-style divisions, or transfers of memories from one brain to another. The answers given to the questions raised by these cases vary. Some say that bodily criteria are the central ones: so long as my body has an uninterrupted path through space and time, that embodied person will still be me, whatever changes in memory and personality I have had. Others say that mental criteria, and particularly memory, are central: if my body or brain cannot survive, but my memories and outlook can be transferred unimpaired to some other body and brain, then *I* have survived in a different body. Yet others say that, in these puzzle cases, the question 'Will it still be me?' does not admit of an all-or-none answer. On this last view, personal survival may be a matter of degree.[6]

If the bodily continuity view of personal identity is the right one, the person on the experience machine will be me. On the other hand, if

6. On these issues, see Sydney Shoemaker: *Self-Knowledge and Self-Identity*, Ithaca, 1963; Derek Parfit: 'Personal Identity', *Philosophical Review* 1971; Bernard Williams: *Problems of the Self*, Cambridge, 1973, chapters 1 and 4; Anthony Quinton: *The Nature of Things*, London, 1973, chapter 4; Amelie Rorty (ed.): *The Identities of Persons*, Berkeley, 1976; David Wiggins: *Sameness and Substance*, Oxford, 1980, chapter 6.

psychological criteria are the ones we ought to invoke, whether or not the person on the machine will be me depends on the answers to questions such as how much memory is left of my life before being plugged in. And, on the last view, this is just another case where we cannot give a yes-or-no answer to the question 'Will it still be me?' So it is not at all clear that going on the machine would be the end of me. And this thought is perhaps bolstered by a negative version of the experience machine, where what is produced is pure nightmare rather than pleasure. Threatened with a lifetime on such a machine, some of us would feel more filled with dread than we would if we knew that some unknown person was to be subjected to this horror. Our inclination seems to be towards the view that we do survive the transition to the machine, at least to some degree.

9 Personal Characteristics

The third identity objection has to do with our desire to have certain characteristics. If I want to be courageous, kind or witty, going on the machine will frustrate these desires, although I will not realize it. My desire is to be courageous, not just to have experiences as though rescuing someone from a burning building, or as though being given the George Medal. Nozick suggests that this identity objection cannot be the whole source of our resistance to the experience machine: 'Imagine a transformation machine which transforms us into whatever sort of person we'd like to be (compatible with our staying us). Surely one would not use the transformation machine to become as one would wish, and thereupon plug into the experience machine! So something matters in addition to one's experiences *and* what one is like.'[7] But, while Nozick is surely right that concern to be a certain sort of person is only part of our objection to the experience machine, it is doubtful if the idea of combining it with the transformation machine is really coherent. This idea seems to presuppose that what you are is quite independent of what you do. If I am a miser who would like to be generous, and so use the transformation machine and then go on the experience machine, where I have many pleasurable experiences as though of giving away money, it is not clear what sort of person I am. Can a visit to the transformation

7. op. cit. p. 44.

machine turn me into a generous person, despite the fact that I never really perform a single generous act? If this doubt is right, and what I am depends on what I do, the experience machine, even supplemented by the transformation machine, is still open to objection on the grounds of the sorts of characteristics we want to have.

The fourth identity objection is that, even if it is allowed that I have these characteristics when on the experience machine, they are not the product of my decisions while on it. For, at most, I have experiences as though I were taking decisions. The reality is one of passive consumption. And this objection is quite correct.

Chapter 8 Dreams (II)

Sooner or later some eminent physiologist will have his neck broken in a super-civilized accident or find his body cells worn beyond capacity for repair. He will then be forced to decide whether to abandon his body or his life. After all, it is brain that counts ...

J. D. Bernal: *The World, the Flesh and the Devil*

Many scientists as well as philosophers have indeed often used the term 'real' in an honorific way to express a value judgement and to attribute a 'superior' status to things judged to be real. There is perhaps an aura of such honorific connotation whenever the word is employed, despite explicit avowals to the contrary and certainly to the detriment of clarity. For this reason it would be desirable to ban the use of the word altogether.

Ernest Nagel: *The Structure of Science*

The objections so far to the experience machine which are worth taking seriously are about other people, about activity, and about identity. It is possible to develop the idea of the experience machine, and, in doing so, to go some way towards meeting these objections.

1 The Dreamworld

Let us first turn the machine into one which allows the person on it to choose between alternatives (the active experience machine). The world presented through the machine would be like one of those films where everything is seen from the perspective of a participant, whose angle of vision is that of the camera. But unlike a film, the sensory experience would not be limited to sight and hearing. Watching a film, I am passive: the camera's movements are independent of my will. The active experience machine would be different. I could decide where to go, and where to look, whether to listen or to block my ears, what to touch, smell or taste. And my decisions would be followed by the appropriate changes in my experience. (I experience myself controlling what I do, but not having magical control over the rest of the world.) In the subjective world of the active experience machine, I control everything I do and say, to the same extent as in the ordinary world. Let us call the experiences offered by such machines 'active dreams'.

In an active dream there are limits on what I can do, just as there are in the ordinary world. Because the point of an experience machine is to provide experiences that are as a whole more satisfactory than those of ordinary life, the limits on what I can do may be less restricting than they are now, but the constraints are still there, even if set in different places. Exceptional achievements by the standards of the active dream will require exceptional effort, determination or concentration.

Let us next have different people on different machines, which are all controlled by a synchronizer. The function of the synchronizer is to coordinate the different active dreams. You have a part to play in the experiences I have, and I have a part in yours. Our decisions affect the parts we play, not only in our own dreams, but in each other's. The synchronizer ensures that when you, in your active dream, come and see me, I experience a visit from you in my dream. Let us call the world presented in these synchronized active dreams the dreamworld.

The synchronization involved in the dreamworld sets limits to the kinds of possible improvements over our ordinary world. This can be seen by asking the question whether people in the dreamworld would be able to act in ways that harm each other. If the answer is 'no', we are back with the drawbacks of behaviour control. We have lost a large range of possible choices, and have correspondingly lost some of the role our choices play in creating our own characteristics. (Being considerate, for instance, would no longer be a characteristic we could freely choose from among other possibilities. The difficulties parallel those in theological discussions of how far God could have made a better world while allowing people freedom.) But suppose the answer is 'yes': that people would still be free to do normal things to each other. We can then see that many of the drawbacks of ordinary life would persist in the dreamworld, in a way that they would not in the simple

103

experience machine. Although this sets limits to the improvement of life in the dreamworld, it does not rule out the possibility of life still being much better than in the ordinary world. In the theological debate, even if we accept the arguments about human freedom offered by God's defence lawyers, we may still want to press questions about why He created earthquakes, diseases and other evils which are independent of human activity. And in creating the dreamworld, it is the experience of these independent evils which would be eliminated in order to make life there more attractive.

Suppose each person in a community is plugged into one of the machines and enters a dreamworld. How far does such a dreamworld meet the objections to the primitive version of the experience machine?

It is tempting to say that all of them are met. The case for this is simple. I am, in the important ways, active. I take decisions in the dreamworld, and put them into effect there. The activity can be quite demanding, because of the constraints on what I can do. And it is not futile, as what I do makes a difference to other people, whose experiences will be affected. When we all enter the dreamworld, I can continue having relationships with the same people as before. There will be no need for a result machine, as I can do in the dreamworld all the things for others I intended to do in the ordinary world. If we retain memories of life before, and a reasonable continuity of character, entering the dreamworld will not be a kind of suicide. Since what I do in the dreamworld will depend a lot on my decisions, there will be scope for having particular characteristics. I can be intelligent or stupid, brave or cowardly, generous or mean. The decisions I take will largely determine the character I have.

When the case is put like this, the dreamworld seems merely to be a different environment, and the idea of having deep objections of principle to it seems no more sensible than having such objections to living in Madagascar. But it may be said that this representation of the dreamworld as a different environment in which I still do the same things is misleading. The objector will say that in the dreamworld we are not really doing things, but only having a kind of collective hallucination that we are active. He will say that the dreamworld, like the simple experience machine, is excellent from the internal perspective. But, from our external perspective, we rejected the simple experience machine because we prefer really doing things to having experiences as if we were doing them. The suggestion is that the dreamworld falls under the same objection: a flexible shared hallucination is still no adequate substitute for reality.

2 Is the Dreamworld Real?

The question of whether the dreamworld meets the objections to the simple experience machine depends on whether we count what goes on in it as really happening. If we do, then the objections about activity, identity and other people are all met. But if we think that the dreamworld is just a shared hallucination, the objections about activity and identity are not all met. How should we decide whether or not the events in the dreamworld really are taking place?

Our normal tests for reality pull two ways here. On the one hand, we usually regard something as real if our own senses agree (it looks and feels like a brick wall) and if we have the support of other people, who say their experience fits with ours. In the dreamworld, we would be in contact with other people in the sense of centres of consciousness. Your thoughts would be communicated to me, and mine to you. If the arrangement included memories of how we entered the dreamworld by hooking up to the machine, and of our life before that, we could come to think of the normal world and the dreamworld merely as alternative environments. We might not regard either as unreal.

But, on the other hand, the causal dependence of the dreamworld on the normal world, combined with the possibility of one day 'waking up', makes us inclined to think of the dreamworld as unreal. A 'world' that is created within, and dependent upon, another one (as the 'world' of a film or a play depends upon our everyday world) is not taken to be real.

The limitations imposed by this causal dependence seem particularly striking when we ask whether or not our projects in the dreamworld could include scientific research. We could have experiences as of being in laboratories and carrying out experiments, and we could think critically and theorize on the basis of the results we seemed to be getting. But, while we remain within the confines of the dreamworld, there is no question of us making empirical discoveries about the ordinary world on which the dreamworld depends. Our 'research' might consist in discovering things about the ordinary world already known to the dreamworld's programmer, but not known to us. Or it might consist in discovering things only 'true' in the dreamworld: solving puzzles set by the programmer, with no relevance to the ordinary world. At best it might consist in theorizing on the basis of true empirical data about the ordinary world, fed in by the programmer. On any of these interpretations, dream-science seems a poor substitute for science, and this reduces our inclination to think of the dreamworld as real.

That inclination is further reduced by thoughts about having children. Suppose a couple and their present children, Adam, Benjamin and Rebecca, all decide to enter the dreamworld. Being able to communicate with each other, they may take the view that the dreamworld is just an alternative medium, no less real than the ordinary world. The couple decide to have more children, and soon the family has been augmented by Ingrid and Ingmar. The whole family knows about having entered the dreamworld, and they remember which things happened before they did so, and which things came afterwards. The parents sometimes have slight feelings of unease about Ingrid and Ingmar. These feelings might be related to the thought that Ingrid and Ingmar are only dreamchildren, not themselves plugged into a machine. When time is short, and Adam and Ingrid both want help with their homework, should they be given equal time? Or is there something wrong with diverting anything from the original children in order to be fair to Ingrid and Ingmar?

Compared with the simple experience machine, the dreamworld has a superior claim to reality, partly because of the coherence of different people's experiences. Adam, Benjamin and Rebecca can share experiences and communicate with each other. But suppose the parents and two of the original children are unplugged, and so leave the dreamworld. Benjamin, the remaining original member, finds his experiences fit exactly with those reported by Ingrid and Ingmar. But he may find this less than completely reassuring.

The points about dreamscience and dreamchildren illustrate the central weakness in the dreamworld's claim to be real. Neither the science nor the children have any independent life of their own. They are products of the programme devised in the ordinary world. The causal dependence they illustrate makes us reluctant to concede the reality of events in the dreamworld.

I said that our tests pull both ways here. The dreamworld provides coherent experiences that different people share. On the other hand, these experiences are explained by their dependence on our ordinary world. When we focus on this dependence, the dreamworld seems no more real than the world of a film. But other reflections push us the other way. It is not like seeing a film from the cinema seat: it is like being a conscious participant in a film where the other characters are conscious too. And this is so unlike anything we have experienced before that we do not have a ready-made answer to the question of whether it is real.

Perhaps in this sort of case, Ernest Nagel's inclination to ban the word 'real' has point. In ordinary life, the various tests we use to find out whether something is real rather than hallucinatory, imaginary, etc. normally converge on the same answer. But the dreamworld divides these tests. In doing so, it casts doubt on whether 'being real' is a unitary matter. We tend to assume that whether or not something is real is a fact, perhaps of a profound kind, for which the results of our tests are evidence. But perhaps there is no fact about the reality of the dreamworld beyond those results. It may be that, when we know about the inter-subjective coherence of the dreamworld, and about its causal dependence on the ordinary world, there is nothing more to know about its reality.

Rather than trying to settle the issue of whether the borderline of the word 'real' should be drawn on one side or the other of the dreamworld, it may be more fruitful to ask what it is that makes the reality of things important to us.

3 Deception, and What We Want

When we want something, say friendship, this is not just a matter of wanting to have a (possibly false) belief that we have friends. Someone's brilliant and sustained pretence that he is my friend may be, from my point of view, subjectively indistinguishable from the reality. Yet, think-ing about the question, I can separate the two possibilities, and have a strong preference for the reality over the pretence. This preference is very common. So, when we are given the subjective experiences that go with the thing desired, it does not follow that we have been given what we want.

A second, related, point is that in general we prefer not to be deceived. Where the world is not as we would wish, we are reluctant to make ourselves more cheerful at the cost of our beliefs becoming divorced from reality. There are cases where some of us do prefer deception, or at least ignorance. Perhaps some people would rather not know that their illness is fatal. But these cases, where 'human kind cannot bear very much reality', only show that some fears or horrors are sufficient to override our normal preference for our beliefs being true and as complete as possible. Perhaps our general concern that our beliefs should not be divorced from reality is partly explained by our wish to avoid unpleasant shocks later, and even more by the importance of true beliefs in guiding effective action. Whatever the explanation, the resistance to distorted beliefs seems an important part of our psychology.

These two points count against the simple version of the experience machine. Many of our desires are not satisfied by it. If I want to make a substantial contribution to physics, my ambition is *not* realized by going on an experience machine which happens to be playing the 'Einstein' cassette. And the satisfaction involved depends on my having a whole system of false beliefs about being Einstein.

But it is doubtful whether these points have any force against the dreamworld. This is because it is not clear that what goes on in the dreamworld is unreal. And so it may be that my desires to do various things are being realized, despite my being in the dreamworld. And, if so, there may be no false beliefs involved, especially if the dreamworld is an 'open' one, where I have full knowledge of having entered the dreamworld, and of my life previous to that. So unless there is some independent way of establishing its unreality, I may not be entitled to object that the dreamworld fails to satisfy my desires in general, or that it goes against my desire not to be deceived.

4 The Objection That the Dreamworld is Mind-Centred

Another source of resistance to the dreamworld, which may underlie criticisms of its 'unreality', is that it is totally mind-centred. In the dreamworld, things only exist for consciousness, and there is no room for anything having any value independent of its contribution to the life of some conscious mind. For many people, there are things whose value is not in this way mind-dependent, and so for them the dreamworld fails to accommodate all they care about. It is worth looking briefly at this line of thought, and at an opposed one, which can be called the mind-dependence view.

The disagreement is not a new one. Henry Sidgwick supported a version of the mind-dependence view when he said, 'No one would consider it rational to aim at the production of beauty in external nature, apart from any possible contemplation of it by human beings.'[1] And G. E. Moore took a strongly opposed view in his comment on Sidgwick:

> Let us imagine one world exceedingly beautiful. Imagine it as beautiful as you can; put into it whatever on this earth you most admire – mountains, rivers, the sea; trees and sunsets, stars and moon. Imagine all these combined in the most exquisite proportions, so that no one thing jars against another, but each contributes to increase the beauty of the whole. And then imagine the ugliest world you can possibly conceive. Imagine it simply one heap of filth, containing everything that is most disgusting to us, for whatever reason, and the whole, as far as may be, without one redeeming feature. Such a pair of worlds we are entitled to compare: they fall within Prof. Sidgwick's meaning, and the comparison is highly relevant to it. The only thing we are not entitled to imagine is that any human being has, or ever, by any possibility. *can*, live in either, can ever see and enjoy the beauty of the one or hate the foulness of the other. Well, even so. supposing them quite apart from any possible contemplation by human beings: still, is it irrational to hold that it is better that the beautiful world should exist, than the one which is ugly? Would it not be well, in any case, to do what we could to produce it rather than the other? Certainly I cannot help thinking that it would; and I hope that some may agree with me in this extreme instance.[2]

(Moore puts the point in terms of human awareness, but it can be generalized to cover minds of any sort. And both Moore and Sidgwick discuss the issue in terms of rationality, which adds an extra complication. When that is eliminated, the mind-dependence issue remains.)

It is hard to see how to argue for or against the mind-dependence view when presented with Moore's alternatives. Neither Sidgwick nor Moore gives us much of an argument: Sidgwick tells us what he thinks no one would consider rational, while Moore tells us what he cannot help thinking. And Moore's thought experiment is problematic. If we feel disgust when we imagine the world full of filth, we may not be

1. *The Methods of Ethics*, Sixth Edition, 1901, Book I, chapter 4. See also Book III, chapter 14, sections 4 and 5.
2. *Principia Ethica*, 1903, pp. 83–4.

quite clear what this is a reaction to. If our imagining it involves having images, we may be disgusted by them (experiences we *are* having) rather than by the possibility of an unseen heap of filth. This is not to make some Berkeleyan point about the impossibility of imagining unperceived things, but to suggest that our discrimination between the different potential objects of our dislike may be too crude for the thought experiment to be reliable.

Perhaps neither Sidgwick nor Moore is irrational or confused. The question is about what we value, and we may not all agree. My sympathies are strongly on the side of Sidgwick here, being quite unmoved by any of the excellences of universes eternally empty of conscious life. But, like Sidgwick and Moore, I have no argument to prove the other attitude wrong. If, travelling in a train through the middle of a ten-mile railway tunnel, I saw a man leaning out of the window into the darkness, I might wonder what he was doing. If it turned out to be G. E. Moore spraying the walls of the tunnel with paint, because painted walls are better than unpainted ones, even if no one ever sees them, I should not be able to prove him irrational. But I should not accept his offer of the use of a second paint spray, except possibly out of politeness.

5 The Mind-Dependence View

The mind-dependence view is strongly opposed to Moore's position. On this view of value, minds are the centre of the universe. That is, the value of anything ultimately derives from its contribution to the lives of conscious minds. Two features of minds are relevant here. Minds have experiences. And minds care about things. The first feature is only important as a condition of the second.

It is important that minds have a subjective side. Take the children in the dreamworld. To use Thomas Nagel's phrase, there is 'something it is like' to be Adam, Benjamin or Rebecca. They know from the inside what it is like to play a game or think of a good joke. But there is nothing it is like to be Ingrid and Ingmar: they have no 'inside'. There is nothing more to them than their contributions to the experiences of the others. On the mind-dependence view, things can be good or bad because of their contribution to the lives of Adam, Benjamin or Rebecca.

But, because Ingrid and Ingmar have no subjective side, mere relationship to them cannot alter the value of anything.

On this view, having subjective experiences is necessary for being a source of value, but it is not sufficient. Minds above a very primitive level have attitudes and responses to what they experience. It is because of this that they are sources of value. Consider a mind that never rose above mere consciousness. It might have a series of visual experiences, but no kind of attitude or emotional response to what it saw. It would be like a conscious television camera. There seems no reason why merely being observed by this mind should confer value on anything. So the mind-dependence view makes minds that care about things the centre of all value.

From this perspective, the rest of the body is a support system for the brain, and the brain is only important because of its connection with mental states. The ordinary world and the dreamworld are alternative media through which minds communicate. What matters is that there is *some* shared world, upon which minds can act, and through which they can make contact with each other.

To some peoole this will seem to involve an absurd downgrading of the body. To them it will seem a view that would only be put forward by some sedentary philosopher, who cared about thinking but not about physical activity. But this is a misunderstanding. The mind-dependence view supports no preference for the passive over the active. An athlete may opt for the dreamworld if the *experiences* involved in athletics are what he values. And the same applies to sex. A couple, having entered the dreamworld, would share all the experiences they now share. The issue is not the crude one suggested by opposing mental and physical activity. It is the more subtle question of what it is we value in activity of either kind.

The mind-dependence view should not be confused with an egoistic version of it which could be called 'moral solipsism': the outlook which puts other people on a par with physical objects, so that they are only of value because of their relationship to *my* mind. This would put Adam, Benjamin and Rebecca on a par with Ingrid and Ingmar, all only of importance because of their role in my experiences and activities. To say that all value derives from the experiences and activities of minds is a variant of the view that, unlike things, people are ends in themselves. And this view does not single out any particular person as more important than others.

111

The mind-dependence view is not the mere platitude that things can only be valued *by* minds: that we care about things while trees and rocks do not. It is a claim about what things are of value, not about where valuing takes place. It is a claim that G. E. Moore disagrees with, while he has no need to deny that things are valued by minds. His mind values episodes in uninhabited universes, while some other minds do not.

My own sympathies are closer to the mind-dependence view than to Moore's view. I would not attach any value to spraying the tunnel walls. This is because of a belief that some contribution to the life of a conscious mind that cares about things is a necessary condition of anything having value. But it does not follow that states of consciousness themselves are the only things of value. It is possible to believe that what matters is a set of conscious activities and relationships between minds, *in a certain context*. This can be brought out by considering a version of the 'mind-centred' objection to the dreamworld which seems persuasive.

6 Claustrophobia

It matters that the dreamworld is causally dependent on our present world. Dreamscience would not be as good as science, and for the human race to settle for dreamscience would be like someone sticking his head into a bag for ever. The claustrophobia we feel at this prospect is because of the value we place on the open-ended quality of human history and human thought. We are part of a universe larger than ourselves, rather than one of our own creation. ('And so they tell us that Anaxagoras answered a man who was raising problems of this sort and asking why one should choose rather to be born than not – "For the sake of viewing the heavens and the whole order of the universe." '[3]) There is so much more to find out, and so much more to affect our lives in ways now unpredictable. We cut off all this if we retreat to a world of our own making, where our present limitations become the permanent boundaries of our world.

The importance of being able to transcend our present limitations, of having an open-ended future larger than ourselves, is not a value very near the surface of our consciousness. This is because we *do* live in a

3. Aristotle, *Eudemian Ethics*, 1216 a 11.

mainly unexplored and only partly understood universe. This value fits our actual position so well that we are not challenged to articulate it. It is a value brought to the surface by a threat such as the dreamworld.

Things are good or bad because of their contribution to the activities and relationships of beings who are conscious and who care about what happens. So the development of consciousness has a central value. Perhaps when we have eliminated misery and horror from the world, the expansion of our consciousness will be our most important project. But this development of consciousness is not something private and passive, which could come from drugs or from the simple experience machine. It is bound up with contacts between people and with activity. It is not something enclosed, which could be provided by the dreamworld. It depends on our growing understanding of a world larger than we are, and on a future not limited by the way we see things now.

Chapter 9 Work

Thus we have been expressly evolved by nature – with all our impulses and deepest instincts – for the purpose of solving the economic problem. If the economic problem is solved, mankind will be deprived of its traditional purpose.

Will this be a benefit? If one believes at all in the real values of life, the prospect at least opens up the possibility of benefit. Yet I think with dread of the readjustment of the habits and instincts of the ordinary man, bred into him for countless generations, which he may be asked to discard within a few decades.

J. M. Keynes: 'Economic Possibilities for Our Grandchildren' (1930)

We are the grandchildren of Keynes. When we look at the economic pressures on most of the people in the world, we find it hard to share his thought that by the year 2030 mankind will be in sight of solving these problems. This is no criticism of Keynes as a prophet. His prediction was carefully qualified: 'Assuming no important wars and no important increase in population, the *economic problem* may be solved, or at least within sight of solution within a hundred years. This means that the economic problem is not – if we look into the future – *the permanent problem of the human race.*'[1]

We know well what has happened to those optimistic assumptions about population and war. And those of us in relatively advanced countries are at least partly aware, some of the time, of the catastrophic effects of economic deprivation in most other countries. When writing about problems of prosperity and technological advance, it should perhaps be said that we now live in a world where many people have their lifespan halved by poverty.

And yet it may be true that the economic problem is not the permanent problem of the human race. If we can avoid nuclear war and

1. 'Economic Possibilities for Our Grandchildren', in *Essays in Persuasion* (1930).

other catastrophes, we are still at an early stage of our history. We may in time find a way of matching resources and population, and a way of sharing what we have so that deprivation is unknown. We may in time find a way of handing over physical and mental drudgery to machines, so that people are liberated from labouring to earn the necessities of life. Then the economic problem *will* be over. If great optimism about this today seems unjustified, despair goes beyond the evidence too. After only two hundred years of putting science to serious use, sections of the population in advanced countries feel little economic pressure. And with luck we have most of our history still ahead of us.

This chapter is about some values involved in one aspect of escaping from the economic problem: handing over work to machines. The issues raised apply more generally to the whole process of liberation from the struggle to stay alive.

The first part of the industrial revolution distorted people's lives by forcing them into mindless labour. The present phase has to be controlled to avoid a different kind of disaster. Most people's work could largely or entirely be replaced by machines now in existence. The worst result of this would be a world where some people stay in employment, with work taking up more of their life than they would ideally choose, while others have no job because machines have replaced them. A society where some sacrifice too much to their jobs, while others are 'redundant', as we bluntly say, is not an attractive one. This worst outcome is made more likely when power is divided between companies concerned to make profits and unions concerned to defend the interests of those already employed.

Although most of us are unclear about the practical steps required, it is not hard to see the outlines of a better response to the replacement of human labour. We can envisage a society where the remaining work would be shared. People would not be redundant if they wanted to contribute. And people in work would devote less of their lives to their jobs, and more to doing things with their family or friends. Part-time jobs are needed for the liberation of mothers who also want to work. This might become the pattern for most of us, and contribute to the liberation of many men too. And, as the numbers of jobs on assembly lines or in low-grade clerical work declined, we would plan to increase the numbers of people trained in medicine, teaching, scientific research, and other fields where having more people can improve results. Whatever the problems of bringing all this about, it is hard to be satisfied with a society where overcrowded classes, or long waiting lists for medical treatment, coexist with substantial unemployment.

The response of sharing work is not enough. At present, work serves (or *should* serve) three functions. There is the production of goods and services we want. There is the provision of an income for those who work. And work provides, or should provide, intrinsic satisfaction.

Let us, as a thought experiment, suppose we have created a society in which machines have taken over the drudgery, and in which the work left is shared. The fruits of that work are also shared. So both unemployment and poverty are unknown. In that society, utopian by present standards, the first two aims of work are realized. We have the needed goods and services, and everyone has an adequate income. As a result, what is now for most people the sharp barrier between work and private life may become much more blurred. The third demand we make on work will come into prominence: the requirement that it should be intrinsically satisfying. People are different and not everyone wants the same from their work. But we do have some idea how to answer the question: what makes work satisfying?

1 Cooperation and Expression

Some people like to work on their own and perhaps the calm absorption of a composer or a sculptor requires isolation. But part of the pleasure of many other kinds of work is cooperation in a shared enterprise. One ingredient of this is that companionship is something we like. But this is not all, as sharing work is often more satisfying than working while someone else stands beside you making conversation. Another aspect is the importance to people of gaining the respect of others doing similar work. Even a sculptor or composer may be glad to work near to others so that mutual criticism and encouragement is possible. And people take pleasure in the shared success of a collaborative enterprise. Because these things are important to us, it matters that work should not all be broken down into isolated components. We do not all envy the tranquil job of a lighthouse keeper.

It is also important to our sense of our own autonomy that, as far as possible, we take the decisions about our work ourselves. The case for workers' control, for decentralization, and for smaller units, is a familiar one. The importance of these things for making work satisfying is obvious, and needs no further emphasis here.

We care about autonomy in most aspects of our lives, but work is one of the areas where it is most important. This is because satisfying work is not just productive, but is also a means of self-expression. We often hope, through our work, to make some difference to the world. And tied in with this is the hope that the difference will somehow express our particular characteristics. This is not to say that most of us have grandiose fantasies about making a difference on the scale of Mao Tsetung, Henry Ford, Einstein or Picasso. It is rather that, just as we are familiar with the way in which the work of even a minor artist is self-expressive, so we should recognize the importance of this for many other kinds of people. Self-expression may be just as central to the work of doctors, carpenters, teachers, gardeners, lawyers, builders, civil servants, nurses, industrialists and chefs. Studs Terkel, in his book *Working*,[2] quotes someone with the apparently unpromising job of a parking-lot attendant:

'I may pull myself up and brace from the wheel, but I never miss that hole. I make that one swing, with one hand, no two hands. And never use the door open, never park a car with the door open. Always I have my head inside the car, lookin' from the backview mirror. That's why they call me Lovin' Al the Wizard, One-Swing Al ... I was one of the best. I didn't care where the hiker was from, you coulda bet money on me. They'd say, "Lover, you never miss." I say, "When I miss, I slip and I don't slip often." ... I didn't care how big the car was, I didn't care how little it was, I never missed my swing.'

2 The Journey, Not the Arrival

Self-expression requires that work makes demands on us. Although in many of us there is the countervailing drag of laziness, we often prefer more demanding to less demanding activities. As John Rawls puts it, 'Human beings enjoy the exercise of their realized capacities (their innate or trained abilities), and this enjoyment increases the more the capacity is realized, or the greater its complexity.'[3] And, as Rawls

2. *Working*, Harmondsworth, 1977.

3. *A Theory of Justice*, Oxford, 1972, p. 426. Rawls points out that Aristotle and Mill made similar remarks.

also indicates, greater complexity allows greater development and expression of personal style: chess allows for more of this than checkers (draughts). But constraints which demand effort can be as important here as the complexity needed to give scope for personal style. We may feel a need to be stretched, so that our commitment and determination find expression, as well as our tastes and style. It would be frustrating rather than exciting to have divine or magical powers, so that a gesture could bring about anything we wanted. There would be no satisfaction in something which, demanding no effort or skill, gave nothing to push against.

Because of this, it is a mistake to think even of those activities which give little room for the expression of personal style only in terms of results. The saying that the journey, not the arrival, matters, may apply to them too. There is an illustration of this in Tove Jansson's agreeable series of children's books about Moomins. One of the characters in the early book *Comet in Moominland* is a Hemulen who regards everything else in life as a series of tiresome interruptions to his main activity of collecting stamps. His absorption keeps him happy, in a mildly cantankerous way. In the next book, *Finn Family Moomintroll*, the Hemulen appears again as a very miserable character. His collecting has been so successful that he has made the transition from being a collector to being the owner of a complete stamp collection. This ruins his life until someone puts him on to collecting plants.

3 Results and Replacement

Although the results of work are not everything, they can still be important. We often care that what we do makes a difference to the world. Think of being a train driver, about to be replaced by a robot control, but whose job is saved by the union. The new arrangement is that you sit operating the levers, but the robot operates an identical set. Most of the time your decisions agree with those of the robot, but where they do not, the robot levers override yours. This work would seem intolerable because it transparently makes no difference to the world, and is at the same time not sufficiently interesting or demanding to be done, like a sport, for its own sake.

We know that there are machines able to out-perform us, not just at simple skills, but also at many complex ones. Some people argue that the highest intellectual feats could never be duplicated by a machine. Whether or not this is true, it is clear that so far we have handed over only a fraction of the mental tasks where they could replace us. Some of the scientific discoveries we take most pride in might have come more easily to suitably programmed machines. (Interpreting X-ray pictures of DNA as a double helix is a case in point.) We can imagine the stage where discoveries come more quickly if a scientist just thinks up the ideas, and leaves a team of computers to do the research. The final point is where the machine turns out to be better than the human brain even at having the ideas and thinking up the research programme.

Perhaps the whole of science will become a field where we are redundant. We could do the work, but the computer sitting next to us would be quicker and better. We enjoy research, so we might decide not to make such machines. (Although the physical presence of the computer makes a psychological difference, the position is essentially the same if we know how to make it, but decide not to do so.) We may keep a lot of intellectual activity for ourselves, but it will be a kind of sport. The computer could solve a problem, but, as we find it enjoyable, we do it ourselves.

This kind of redundancy might not seem important. People who try to improve their tennis are not worried by the thought that some tennis-playing machine might be much better than they are. (Two such machines might keep up a rally for ever, but after a while the spectators might start to lose interest.) Most scientists are now, as individuals, replaceable by other people. Some great feats of the scientific imagination may not be like this, but in much of science, if one team had not found something out, the overwhelming probability is that some other group would have done. The fact that most scientists are unworried by their replaceability is encouraging. Perhaps, when we have become replaceable, we will adapt to the idea that the exercise of skill is something done for its own sake. We can imagine a mixed policy, where discoveries urgently needed for eliminating some disease would be made more rapidly by machines, while theoretically more absorbing fields with less urgent applications, such as astronomy, would be left for our intellectual sport. (In all this, I assume we do not consider our highly intelligent machines to be conscious, and so do not worry about giving them a fair share of interesting work.)

Our concern to make a difference, to contribute something to the world, is not always threatened by the possibility of replacement. Some painters, novelists, poets, musicians and a few others are in their professional life irreplaceable. For many others, the work they do could be done by someone else, and yet it can still seem satisfying enough. If I help some friends shovelling snow, everything I contribute would have been brought about by the others if I had not been there. Yet, although I am replaceable, I can still feel the satisfaction of making a contribution. What I contribute means that less work is needed from the others. In the case of the replaceable pieces of scientific research, the claim must be that my doing it, while not lightening anyone's burden, releases other scientists to do different work. But this will no longer apply when all the work can be done by available machines. Then the claim about making a difference will have to be scaled down to the more modest one that the end is desirable, whether or not it could be brought about without me.

If our desire to contribute is partly to make a contribution which is in principle unique, this is already unrealistic for most of us, outside relationships. Our present machines' great-grandchildren will only make this far clearer. We will still be able to contribute in the limited sense of doing something which is wanted, even if our doing it is replaceable. The more grandiose picture, of being irreplaceable in principle, will have to be confined almost entirely to relationships. And, even in relationships, our unique contribution is threatened if we contemplate the science-fiction possibility of producing new people who are, in every detail, even down to apparent memories, duplicates of existing people. Confronted with this possibility, some people are tempted by a very strong form of belief in irreplaceability. This is the thought that our contribution to the world depends on something other than our, perhaps reproducible, empirical pattern of abilities and character traits. This rests on the idea that I am a disembodied self, which could have 'owned' a totally different set of physical and psychological characteristics. It also presupposes that this self contributes something additional to the contribution made by the set of empirical characteristics that belong to it. So the science-fiction duplicates of me, having all my physical and psychological features, will not be able to substitute for me in relationships, because they will not *be* me. But, sadly for this most ambitious form of the desire to make a unique contribution, the whole line of thought is misguided. The theory of the disembodied self, detachable from all empirical characteristics, is irredeemably obscure. Even if we could understand the idea, such a self, just as a result of having no empirical features, could make no detectable impact on the world.

There seems little reason why we should ever want to produce duplicate persons. But there are obvious reasons for producing machines which match or surpass our skills. If we think of this possibility only, it is clear that our conception of ourselves as making a unique contribution will need to be modified. The sphere of our uniqueness will be relationships. Work and relationships overlap, but, apart from this, almost all work will be in the sphere of replaceability. It will be done for its intrinsic enjoyment, rather than because our participation is essential. Its satisfactions will be all those which do not depend on inflated beliefs about our own indispensability.

4 Circles

Part of the anxiety about replaceability is the fear that it may make our work meaningless. The train driver, whose job is reduced to acting redundantly in parallel with the robot, may rightly feel that his working life has become pointless. It starts to resemble the circular life of Sisyphus, condemned for ever to roll a stone to the top of a hill, where it rolls down for him to start his labour again. But activity may not become meaningless simply because of the possibility of replacement. The work of the train driver and of Sisyphus have a special futility, setting them apart from many other jobs where we could be replaced. Perhaps Watson and Crick, in discovering the structure of DNA, were doing what we could now make a machine do. We do not as a result class their work with that of Sisyphus. Replaceability and futility are not the same. What is the difference?

Variety is important to us. Part of what is terrible about Sisyphus is the extreme narrowness of the circle he is confined to. And it makes a difference to the train driver's life if he is on a varied and beautiful mountain route with many complex junctions, or if he is on the Circle Line on the London underground. But where the fundamental activity is pointless, variety is only a mitigation, and not a redemption. The work of Sisyphus becomes more tolerable if each hill is a new one, with obstacles needing new kinds of ingenuity. But it would still be discouraging to be advised to take it up as a career.

It also makes a difference if what we are doing is a contribution to something larger than ourselves. Sticking stamps on thousands of envelopes may not seem a task for Sisyphus if we know it is helping the Church or the Party. Work may have more point if it fits into some great cause. But the larger context is not always necessary. A family spends a few days cycling on Romney Marsh. This is not part of a larger project. It is quite enough that it is something they want to do. This suggests that perhaps what stops activity being futile is simply that we want to do it. From an unsympathetic perspective, anyone's life can look like that of Sisyphus. We eat and rest in order to be able to work, and we work in order to earn money for food and rest, and so on. The circles of our lives may seem to differ from those of Sisyphus only in complexity. But this *is* an unsympathetic description, and what it leaves out is our wanting to do many of the activities that come up in the circle.

This line of thought has been developed by Richard Taylor.[4] He suggests that we consider a modified version of the life of Sisyphus. In this, Sisyphus has a compulsive desire to roll stones. Taylor at first seems sympathetic to the view that this does not give any more point to what is still the same endless cycle of futile activity. But later he says that this version of Sisyphus should not be dismissed so briskly. He suggests that our lives are like that of Sisyphus, but that, 'at the same time, the strange meaningfulness they possess is that of the inner compulsion to be doing just what we were put here to do, and to go on doing it for ever'.

This idea, that the point of an activity must ultimately come from our own desires and interests, is right. In many cases, the criticism that what someone is doing is pointless can be met by the reply that he simply wants to do it. And, even where an activity is given point by its contribution to something larger than ourselves, not any larger project will do. As Thomas Nagel has pointed out, our lives would not seem to have more point if we discovered that other beings were rearing us for food.[5] The larger context has to be one we can identify with or

4. In *Good and Evil*, New York, 1970, chapter 18.

5. 'The Absurd', *Journal of Philosophy* 1971, reprinted in his *Mortal Questions*, Cambridge, 1979.

endorse. Isolated actions or larger projects are only saved from futility by our wanting to carry them out. But our desires, while necessary, are not sufficient.

5 Negative Circles

That our wanting to do something may not save it from futility can be seen by considering the melancholy account of human motivation given by Pascal. He said,

Sometimes when I set to thinking about the various activities of men, the dangers and troubles which they face at Court, or in war, giving rise to so many quarrels and passions, daring and often wicked enterprises and so on, I have often said that the sole cause of man's unhappiness is that he does not know how to stay quietly in his room. A man wealthy enough for life's needs would never leave home to go to sea or besiege some fortress if he knew how to stay at home and enjoy it ...

But after closer thought, looking for the particular reasons for all our unhappiness now that I knew its general cause, I found one very cogent reason in the natural unhappiness of our feeble mortal condition, so wretched that nothing can console us when we really think about it ... The only good thing for men therefore is to be diverted from thinking of what they are ... That is why gaming and feminine society, war and high office are so popular. It is not that they really bring happiness, nor that anyone imagines that true bliss comes from possessing the money to be won at gaming or the hare that is hunted: no one would take them as a gift. What people want is not the easy peaceful life that allows us to think of our unhappy condition, nor the dangers or war, nor the burdens of office, but the agitation that takes our mind off it and diverts us. That is why we prefer the hunt to the capture. That is why men are so fond of hustle and bustle; that is why prison is such a fearful punishment; that is why the pleasures of solitude are so incomprehensible.[6]

Pascal is persuasive about our preferring the hunt to the capture, and perhaps hustle and bustle are partly means of avoiding staying quietly in our room. He is less convincing that gaming, feminine society, war and high office are popular only as a distraction from thoughts of death. We have other motives too. But let us think what it would be like if Pascal were right in saying that the *only* good thing for men

6. Pascal: *Pensées*, translated by A. J. Krailsheimer, Harmondsworth, 1966.

is to be diverted from thinking of what they are. Our only motives for action would be negative. We would want to do all the things we now want to do, but only to kill time. We would hunt, make love, fight battles or compete for office, but only to deaden the pain of consciousness. These activities would be as desirable as taking an aspirin to deaden a headache. Our state would be on a par with that of someone for whom we might now think death a mercy: a person in such pain that his whole life is devoted to maintaining his supply of a drug. That kind of life is pointless. So the fact that we want to do things is not enough. The desire must be positive, not the negative aim of avoiding something disliked. If the circles of our life were *only* motivated by negative desires, we would be no worse off unconscious, or even dead.

To avoid futility, positive desires are necessary: but they are not sufficient. Sisyphus, modified by the compulsive desire to roll stones, may not feel as optimistic about his life as Richard Taylor does. If he is happy to have this dominant desire, he will perhaps think his activity worthwhile. But he may not identify with the desire. He may try psycho-analysis or behaviour therapy to get rid of it. Where we are motivated by a positive desire, but the desire itself is one we would as soon be rid of as satisfy, we have only a more subtle version of a negative circle. What we do may seem as pointless as in the cruder version.

We need positive desires, and they must be ones we can identify with. There is the view that even this is not enough to silence doubts about whether our activities have any point. One such line of thought is expressed by Thomas Nagel. He says that 'humans have the special capacity to step back and survey themselves, and the lives to which they are committed, with that detached amazement which comes from watching an ant struggle up a heap of sand. Without developing the illusion that they are able to escape from their highly specific and idio-syncratic position, they can view it *sub specie aeternitatis* – and the view is at once sobering and comical.' Nagel explains how this scepticism about our lives arises: 'We step back to find that the whole system of justification and criticism, which controls our choices and supports our claim to rationality, rests on responses and habits that we never question, and that we should not know how to defend without circularity, and to which we shall continue to adhere even after they are called into question.'[7]

7. Nagel, op. cit.

It is true that justifications have to come to an end somewhere. Every one of our beliefs, whether about what is worth doing or about what the world is like, can be questioned. And, in defending it, we have to draw on the resources of other parts of our system of beliefs. If you question my belief that smoking causes cancer, I will give you some evidence. If you doubt that the issue should be settled by evidence, I may have to explain the role of evidence in science, and mention the success of science in telling us what the world is like. But if you share none of these beliefs, either about the world, or about how to investigate it, evidence and reasoning will make no impact on you. I will be unable to convince you. Scepticism about *all* the beliefs someone holds gives him no possibility of defending his system.

The same applies to doubts about our beliefs about what is worthwhile. If we construct a detached perspective from which to view those beliefs, we will be unable to defend them against scepticism from that position. But perhaps this should not worry us. *This* perspective has been constructed precisely by eliminating all beliefs that anything is worth doing. It is a possible perspective, just as scepticism about all our scientific beliefs is. But the mere possibility of a sceptical perspective need not move us at all. A painter may know some philistine person who thinks all art is rubbish. This gives him no reason to weaken his own commitment to painting. We need defer to some other view only where it reveals some limitation or bias in our own. This holds for the sceptical view of our activities only if our own commitments are limitations or biases. The case for seeing all our concerns as being limited or biased by comparison with an attitude of total detachment needs more supporting argument than it has ever been given.

We can escape from a negative circle by having some positive desires that we identify with. And a life which escapes in this way from being merely negative need not have its point undermined by the possibility of a totally detached viewpoint. But it does not follow from this that any such life will seem worthwhile from our own present position. This can be seen by considering another variant of Sisyphus.

The original Sisyphus had a life of hell, condemned for ever to roll stones. Sisyphus Mark Two was not so straightforwardly in Hell, as he wanted to roll stones. But he was still trapped in a negative circle if he would have preferred to give up both the desire and the activity. Sisyphus Mark Three escapes from a negative circle. Genetic engineering, or behaviour therapy, has made him the kind of person who both wants to roll stones and is pleased to have this dominant desire. Although he escapes from the negative circle, his life is not one which we, with our values, need admire. From our point of view, there is still nothing much to be said for trying to become like him, and much to be said against it.

6 Systems

We have seen some of the values implicit in the idea of worthwhile work. They are cooperation, self-expression, being stretched, and making a contribution to the world. Underlying these is the idea of activity performed for its own sake, motivated by a positive desire with which we can identify. These values can play two roles in decisions about our future. They can be just an uplifting irrelevance, like talk about 'improving the quality of life' tacked on to a political manifesto. Or they can be taken seriously, in the belief that whether human activity can avoid being futile is of some importance. If taken seriously, they change the debate about the aims of an economic system.

Some familiar issues about economic growth have been at the centre of that debate. Critics stress the social and environmental costs of growth, and the pressure put on scarce resources. They sometimes also question whether more goods lead to greater happiness. Defenders of growth say it is necessary for better housing, for better standards in health and education, and for the elimination of poverty. The debate often takes place at a primitive level, because it is assumed that the only choices are to be 'for' or 'against' growth.

The first step towards a more sophisticated discussion is to distinguish between different components of growth. If cars are made to last only half their present lifespan, twice as many may be sold. This is growth, but there may be no benefit to anyone. But growth can also include the mass production of equipment needed for medical diagnosis, which may make us healthier or save our lives. As one of the aims of an economic policy, growth directed towards what people want is more defensible than random growth.

The second step is to recognize that some of the hopes people place in economic growth are self-defeating. This is because, as Fred Hirsch has argued,[8] the value to us of some of the things we want depends on not many other people having them. The value of a weekend cottage in the country depends on how much the view is spoilt by other people having weekend cottages. If higher education is partly valued as a route to the best jobs, its value will be reduced if it is made available to more people. This 'social scarcity', as Hirsch calls it, applies not only to the products of an economic system, but also to other things people want, such as high status. (Imagine the project of expanding *Who's Who* to include everyone.) Hirsch argues that, as well as material goods, there are 'positional goods': those which in this way depend on what other people have. The suggestion is that many of the things people want from economic growth are unrecognized positional goods, and that this is why the results of growth often seem less satisfying than was hoped. As Hirsch puts it, 'if everyone stands on tiptoe, no one sees better'. So, in deciding what to create more of, we have to avoid self-defeating attempts to give everyone benefits which are positional. Once a system is set up, it can be rational for each person to compete within it. If a Ph.D. is made a requirement for the best jobs, each of us has a motive for writing a thesis we might otherwise think pointless. And demand for graduate places creates pressure for more to be funded. Although each of us has a reason to participate, it would be better if the whole cycle had never started. We are worse off when we all end up on tiptoe.

It is possible for an economic system to avoid self-defeating goals, and to be directed towards giving people what they want, and yet to be open to the criticism of futility. This is made more likely when the system not only satisfies desires, but also shapes them. We can imagine a society where people in their role as producers are persuaded by financial inducements and by 'personnel managers' to want to produce goods, which the same people in their role as consumers are then persuaded by advertising to want to buy. (Imagine?)

This production–consumption circle is one where most activity would have merely instrumental value. Working for money, and buying things because we think they will impress the neighbours, we would come close to what Bertrand Russell once called 'worldliness'. He wrote, in a letter to Colette Malleson, 'I want to stand ... against worldliness, which consists of doing everything for the sake of something else, like marrying

8. *Social Limits to Growth*, London, 1977.

127

for money instead of love. The essence of life is doing things for their own sakes ...'[9]

A satisfactory economic system must at least avoid this kind of 'worldliness': there must be some things and activities desired and chosen for their own sakes. And there are requirements beyond this: the desires must be ones that people are glad to have. Otherwise they are in a negative circle, like Sisyphus Mark Two. And, even where those in a society identify with their desires, this may not be enough to persuade *us*, viewing it from outside, that the system is a good one. We may still regard it as a case of Sisyphus Mark Three. But at least such a society satisfies the minimum condition, that what people do has some justification beyond being a contribution to a negative circle.

7 Transcending the Economic Problem

Wars and over-population, as Keynes saw, may stop us solving the economic problem. Both can (at least) keep us back where we are now, with most of the human race having lives below any acceptable material minimum.

Even if we avoid war, limit our population, and find abundant resources, we can still prolong the economic problem. We may fail to see positional goods for what they are, and so demand production of more of the things which leave us still frustrated when we have them. Or, even if we understand about social scarcity, we can prolong the economic problem by locking ourselves into a system requiring the endless generation of new desires for goods.

If we reach the stage where, in material terms, everyone has an acceptable life, we will not thereby have eliminated the economic problem. That will require a further decision. We will be able to choose whether to prolong or to transcend that problem. Because we can always create new demands for goods, it is possible for the whole future of our species to centre round the cycle of production and consumption. The alternative is to relegate goods to the background, and to make activities and relationships the central focus of life. The boring, unsatisfying tasks would be given to machines. But, although machines could replace us, we

9. Quoted in Ronald W. Clark: *The Life of Bertrand Russell*, Harmondsworth, 1978, p. 436.

would not hand over those things which we like doing for their intrinsic satisfaction. Economics would be largely about arranging things so that people could express themselves in freely chosen work. The decision to shift the emphasis from goods to activity is not the kind to be taken by some government on a particular day. Rather it may slowly emerge as attitudes change. But if we do take that decision, the obsession with 'standard of living' will then be over, and the liberated stage of our history will begin.

Chapter 10 Thoughts on the
Thought Experiments

The thought experiments have some obvious limitations. There has been a high degree of abstraction from social context. The kinds of activity found satisfying may depend on whether 'work' and 'leisure' are still distinct compartments of life, and on which aspects of us the educational system tries to draw out. Attitudes to privacy will vary according to whether there are governments, and, if so, whether people are afraid of them. This also holds for responses to the technology of altering desires, moods and experiences. And all the choices will be influenced by prevailing systems of belief, as well as by the machinery for taking social and political decisions.

All this has been left out. As a result, the thought experiments may seem to have the thin unreality of science fiction. The criticism is that real choices are not about single technologies in isolation. There are complicated relationships between social, political, economic and technological changes taking place at the same time. The values that influence the choices are themselves the product of a given society at a particular time. The thought experiments lack the historian's perspective.

The point about the artificiality of the thought experiments is quite correct. It would be a devastating objection if they had been intended to provide a plan for a future utopia. But the aim has been different. Thought experiments are *experiments*, and have the same kind of artificial exclusions as those that take place in science. To rule out the possibility that a study of the effect of a drug is being biased by the age, sex or medical history of the people who take it, scientists use a control group matched for these features. If I try to find out the value you place on privacy by asking you about some actual proposal, such as a National Health Service data bank containing medical records of everyone in the country, your answers may not tell me what I want to know. They may be influenced by your belief that doctors take inaccurate notes, or by your fear that the Home Office might gain access to the records and use them for some illiberal purpose. To control for these factors, it is necessary to describe an imaginary case which excludes them. Thought experiments are designed to elicit people's values. Bare and abstract description is the way of controlling for the biases which would be generated by the details of more realistic accounts.

The parallel with science should not be exaggerated. The norm in science is for issues to be resolved by objective tests, and there is usually enough agreement on what the tests should be for a consensus to emerge on the issue in question. (This is not to deny the point, seized upon and much exaggerated by some philosophers of science, that the evidence of observation and experiment may often admit of different interpretations.) The use of thought experiments to elicit people's values may lead to no such consensus. This is not because of some inadequacy in the technique, but because people's values differ. Perhaps you are much more opposed to intervention to change people's natural brain chemistry than I am. Or perhaps I care more about autonomy than you do. There is no reason to expect unanimity on these issues. And, where we disagree, it may not be that one of us is in some way mistaken. People in disagreement on a scientific matter rightly suppose that at least one of them must be wrong. The world cannot be such that, for a given population in a given environment, smoking both does and does not increase the risk of lung cancer. But people whose values conflict are not in the same position. There seems to be no external reality to appeal to for adjudication. If you think equality is more important than liberty, while I disagree (to present a crudely over-simplified case), it is not clear what could be meant by the suggestion that one of us is closer to the *real* rank ordering.

The thought experiments have not been used in an attempt to demonstrate that certain values are shared by us all, or that they would be shared by all fully rational people. It has been suggested that a set of values does emerge from them, but the values reflect my responses to these possibilities, and your responses may often be different. If I had thought my responses were so idiosyncratic that they would only rarely coincide with other people's, there would have been little point in giving them. I hope the position is not as bad as that, and the conclusions drawn can be seen not only as an expression of my attitudes, but as a conjecture about those of a fair number of other people. In this way, the discussion can be seen as a kind of *a priori* psychology. Of course, psychology is an empirical subject, and ultimately such questions as how many people share all or some of these values, how differences of value come about, and how people's values change, are to be answered by empirical investigation. But it would be absurd to say that, before psychologists have done their studies, we know nothing about the values of ourselves and others. We see how other people act, and we talk to them. And the studies of psychologists must partly consist in asking us about our values. Because of the conjecture that a fair number of people will have responded to the thought experiments in ways that overlap with the responses given here, I shall write of 'our' values, but this is subject to all the qualifications about disagreement that have been expressed.

The thought experiments have not been designed to bring out all our values, but only those that are particularly relevant to deciding what use should be made of biotechnology and of intelligent machines. And the values that have emerged are far from being the constant preoccupation of our lives. From day to day we may be busy with a job, taking the children to school, arranging a holiday in Italy, or getting the plumbing mended. There would be something absurd about constantly thinking about grand projects of self-creation across a lifetime, or about the need for self-expression in work. Some of these values are in most of us rather deeply buried, and perhaps only readily become articulated when they are threatened, as they are in some of the thought experiments. Some of our values, such as justice, or political liberty, or our revulsion against cruelty, are highly visible because the present world is one in which they are affronted daily. But other values, the ones discussed here, are less subject to immediate affronts and threats. We are not going to have the experience machine next year, and so we are hardly aware of the value we place on genuine contact with other people, or on both physical and mental activity. (Just as most of us, who are neither mountaineers nor pilots, only value the oxygen in the air we breathe on rare moments when we think of it.) The aim of the thought experiments has been to bring these unnoticed background values into the foreground, and to bring them into sharper focus. And the picture which has emerged is one in which our values turn out to be very different from the simple materialism often presupposed by schemes for economic advance.

What I hope has emerged is a set of values centred on people (in a broad sense which may include members of other species, and inhabitants of other planets). People have this central position because they are conscious and care about things. Three aspects of people's lives have been suggested to be both important and threatened by some of the possible technologies. These are: self-development and self-expression; certain kinds of contact with other people; the development of consciousness.

1 Self-Development and Self-Expression

We care about what sort of people we are, wanting to have skills or personal qualities some of which we could not have on the simple experience machine. We do not want individuality to be curbed by the sorts of pressures that could arise in a world where we were transparent to each other. But it is not just a matter of wanting to have certain characteristics, and particularly ones that mark us off from other people. We want our development, at least in part, to be a reflection of our own choices and values. At each stage of life, we are partly the creation of our earlier selves. This is something we value, and do not want to hand over to benevolent controllers, whether human or mechanical, whether they use brain stimulation or drugs to alter our desires or experiences. On the other hand, this is a reason for welcoming technology giving us greater control over our own desires.

This project of self-creation is expressed in activity. This is why work is important to us in ways that go beyond its economic results. To express ourselves, we need control over what we do, in a way that is impossible for the passive consumer of a programme on the simple experience machine. And the activity has to be wanted for its own sake rather than part of a negative circle: there is little self-expression in taking an aspirin to avoid a headache. And the further requirement, that the positive desire is one we identify with, is also bound up with self-expression. A desire we would as happily eliminate as satisfy plays no part in our project of self-creation.

2 Contact and Variety

We mind about having contact with other people to such an extent that, for some of us, this alone is enough to rule out the simple experience machine, however great its other advantages. And, whatever reservations we have about a world of transparent relationships, some of us can see real advantages in the shared understanding it would bring.

We value not only contact with others, but also activity that is shared, where we can contribute to each other's projects. But we also want their projects very often not to overlap with ours, perhaps even to conflict with ours, because we want many different styles of life and ways of seeing the world to exist and be expressed. We are not attracted by cloning, or by any world where psychological technology has increased conformity. And our relationships with each other depend on the interlocking of our individual responses (shared or contrasting). So we are wary of drugs designed to 'improve' our emotional state in detachment from our beliefs and our perception of things.

3 The Development of Consciousness

Consciousness is central to our system of values, but is focused on a world outside itself. Blissful states of consciousness are not all we care about. We resist the simple experience machine because we do not want to have beliefs that are systematically false. Even the dreamworld seems stifling because we want a world bigger than ourselves to explore.

But consciousness is the centre of value. We do not value an uninhabited world, of whatever size and complexity. We want a world transcending ourselves because of the opportunity it gives for the development of our awareness and understanding, in ways now unpredictable.

(As the writer of this book on philosophy, I feel unease about a value system giving such prominence to intellectual activity. So many people think the universe centres on what they do. The possibilities of professional deformation and self-deception are obvious. Sometimes it seems that interest in philosophy, literature, the arts, or the more theoretical parts of science is a luxury: the product of a material comfort not shared by most of the people in the world. Relative freedom from material worries, which lets people write books, is the product of other people's work. Even if conditions down mines have changed, George Orwell's point remains true:

In a way it is even humiliating to watch coal miners working. It raises in you a momentary doubt about your own status as an 'intellectual' and a superior person generally. For it is brought home to you, at least while you are watching, that it is only because miners sweat their guts out that superior persons can remain superior. You and I and the editor of the *Times Lit. Supp.*, and the poets and the Archbishop of Canterbury and Comrade X, author of *Marxism for Infants* – all of us *really* owe the comparative decency of our lives to poor drudges underground, blackened to the eyes, with their throats full of coal dust, driving their shovels forward with arms and belly muscles of steel.[1]

Writers, philosophers and artists eat food that others have grown and use energy that others have worked to provide, and perhaps do not think enough about the value of what is given back. This line of thought tends to push intellectual activity low down the list of priorities, as the marginal luxury of the comfortable. But I hope that some of the considerations suggested by the thought experiments will partly check this tendency. These activities are not a dispensable frill, but are central to some of the values that give life a focus and a centre, once basic needs for food, shelter and health have been satisfied. *Some* of the values – relationships between men and women, parents and children, which can be of a quite unintellectual kind – are at least as important. But even here, relationships change with ways of thinking and seeing. So, if writers and others do interesting work, perhaps something is given back. Though this too may be self-deception.)

Suppose Stone Age men had been given an opportunity to have the happiest life they could imagine, but at the cost of giving up any chance of further intellectual or emotional development. (The choice could not have been put to them in these terms, but this does not affect the point.) We may think, from our perspective, that accepting this offer would have been a disaster far beyond anything they could understand. And, when we consider handing over control of our brains to machines designed by us now, we cannot tell *what* expansion of consciousness we are giving up. But we can understand that there is such a loss, and so we are reluctant to accept any modern equivalent of the Stone Age offer. We hope that machines will liberate us from the cycle of production and consumption. But we want to be liberated for, not from, new kinds of activity and understanding.

1. 'Down the Mine' (1937), in *Inside the Whale and Other Essays*, Harmondsworth, 1962.

4 Beyond Conservatism about Human Nature

With each of the technologies considered, whether genetic engineering or the developments in the thought experiments, there are many obvious surface objections and dangers. Genetic engineering may involve mistakes or large-scale accidents. Brain technology may involve exploitation by bad governments or for profit.

Below these obvious surface objections is often a conservatism about human nature, which was rejected in the discussion of genetic engineering. Suppose we give up this idea that any major change in what we are like is to be resisted. We then open up possibilities of behaviour control, thought reading, brain stimulation and other such techniques. It is by looking at the deeper reasons for the mixture of fear and occasional hope which these inspire that we come on values whose defence is not mere conservatism. It is not just *any* aspect of present human nature that is worth preserving. Rather it is especially those features which contribute to self-development and self-expression, to certain kinds of relationships, and to the development of our consciousness and understanding. And some of these features may be extended rather than threatened by technology. This applies to devices where we operate directly on the brain to alter our own desires.

If these are some of our values, we can be guided by them in welcoming or opposing the developments scientists will offer us. We may for once have some idea of what we do and do not want before the technology is irreversibly with us. Yet there is a remaining source of unease. These, perhaps, are *our* values. But genetic engineering and the other techniques open up the possibility of producing a world of people with very different values. We may not like some of these possible worlds. But their inhabitants might prefer them. To what extent should decisions about future generations be taken in the light of our present values and outlook? This is the question of the last part of the book.

Part Three: Values

It was recognized that the whole pre-revolutionary population
was afflicted with serious mental diseases, with endemic plagues of
delusion and obsession, due to mental malnutrition and poisoning. As
psychological insight advanced, the same kind of interest was aroused
by the old psychology as is wakened in modern Europeans by ancient
maps which distort the countries of the world almost beyond
recognition.

Olaf Stapledon: *Starmaker*

Chapter 11 Generations

It is helpful to imagine cavemen sitting together to think up what, for all time, will be the best possible society and then setting out to institute it. Do none of the reasons that make you smile at this apply to us?

Robert Nozick: *Anarchy, State and Utopia*

These technologies, with their threats and promises, will affect future people more than us. Obviously genetic engineering will affect only future people, and the applications of neurobiology will be greater when the brain is better understood than now. How far should this alter our thinking about these issues? How much, if at all, should we take account of the interests of future generations? If we do give some weight to their interests, in what ways should we do so?

1 Stalin and Herzen

Attitudes have varied all the way from the view that the interests of future generations should largely override those of people now alive, to the opposite opinion that we need give future people no consideration at all. In the days of Stalin, part of the propaganda for his activities appealed to the future. It was said that the horrors imposed by his rule on that generation of Russians were justified by huge benefits to later generations. The supposed causal connections linking extermination and terror with the future benefits were only apparent to the eyes of the faithful. So that defence of Stalin is rightly discredited. And, rather as a proper revulsion against Nazism has often spilled over into hostility to all policies of eugenics or euthanasia, so the reaction against Stalinism has led to scepticism about any sacrifices for future generations.

These doubts were given their most forceful expression, long before Stalin, by Alexander Herzen:

If progress is the end, for whom are we working? Who is this Moloch who, as the toilers approach him, instead of rewarding them, only recedes, and as a consolation to the exhausted, doomed multitudes crying '*morituri te salutant*', can give back only the mocking answer that after their death all will be beautiful on earth. Do you truly wish to condemn all human beings alive today to the sad role of caryatids supporting a floor for others some day to dance on ... or of wretched galley slaves, up to their knees in mud, dragging a barge filled with some mysterious treasure and with the humble words 'progress in the future' inscribed on its bows? Those who are exhausted fall in their tracks; others with fresh forces take up the ropes; but there remains, as you said yourself, as much ahead as there was at the beginning, because progress is infinite. This alone should serve as a warning to people: an end that is infinitely remote is not an end, but, if you like, a trap ...[1]

The view that the interests of present people should always count for less than those of future people has little attraction. It is unfair: why should our lives and happiness matter less, just because we live now rather than in two hundred years' time? It involves an absurd degree of confidence in our predictions: how do we know what the world will be like in a few generations' time, or what people then will want? Applied in every generation, it has the danger of the paradox which Herzen pointed out, that if every generation makes the sacrifices, the benefits are deferred for ever. So, quite apart from Stalinist associations, policies of heroic self-sacrifice by present people are open to obvious criticism. But, where people have a normal amount of selfishness, heroic self-sacrifice is likely to have little support. It would be perverse to make the weaknesses of that policy the centre of discussion. In practice, decisions are more likely to reflect the view that future generations have little or no claim on us. The serious debate is between that view and some alternative more plausible than endlessly repeated self-sacrifice. One such alternative gives equal weight to people's interests, whichever generation they belong to.

2 The Equality Principle

This principle that people's interests should be given equal weight, regardless of their generation, is a rejection of one kind of dis-

1. *From the Other Shore*, translated by Moura Budberg, Oxford, 1979, pp. 36–7. Like many others, I first came across Herzen's ideas through the writings of his distinguished modern follower Isaiah Berlin.

crimination, of one way of departing from impartiality. The belief that people should be given equal consideration, or should be treated equally unless there is some relevant difference between them, has been argued for by various thinkers in different ways. It is sometimes said that this impartiality is built into either the concept of morality or the concept of justice.

One such argument is found in the writings of R. M. Hare,[2] who claims that universalizability is a logical feature of moral judgements: if I believe that you ought (morally) to give away half your income, I am logically committed to holding that anyone else in relevantly similar circumstances ought to do the same thing. Hare argues that this property of moral beliefs generates an impartial utilitarian morality, in which everyone's interests are given equal weight. In deciding what we ought to do, we have to place ourselves in turn in the position of everyone affected by the different courses of action, whichever generation they belong to.

A rather similar conclusion is reached by John Rawls,[3] who appeals to the concept of justice. In his well-known theoretical model, the impartiality required by justice is secured by working out the terms of the contract which would be agreed between self-interested and rational people ignorant of which position in society they are to occupy. Rawls applies his model to the case of justice between generations by stipulating that the people making the contract all belong to the same generation, but do not know which one it is. He thinks this procedure would generate a 'just savings principle', and says, 'We can now see that persons in different generations have duties and obligations to one another just as contemporaries do. The present generation cannot do as it pleases but is bound by the principles that would be chosen in the original position to define justice between persons at different moments of time.'[4]

Both Hare and Rawls derive their conclusions from more general theories that are controversial. Hare's theory depends on linguistic intuitions about the meanings of words used in making moral judgements. Some of Hare's critics disagree with his claims about moral language. Others disagree with his derivation of impartial utilitarianism from the universalizability of moral judgements. And others say that, if the use of moral

2. *Freedom and Reason*, Oxford, 1963.
3. *A Theory of Justice*, Oxford, 1972, especially section 44.
4. ibid., p. 293.

language commits us to utilitarianism, they will abandon it and use non-moral terms to express their non-utilitarian values. There is scepticism about an argument ruling out all systems of values but one, and whose authority ultimately rests at least in part on claims about the meanings of words.[5]

Rawls bases his theory on claims about what he calls 'reflective equilibrium': a state where our theoretical views and our intuitive responses to particular cases have been adjusted to each other in such a way that they form a stable system. Our intuitive beliefs about what is just are in part to be corrected by the results of the theoretical model. But the terms of the 'original position' in which the rational contractors reach their agreement are also adjusted to bring the results close to our intuitive ideas of justice. As the contractors all belong to the same generation, there seems no reason why their agreement should include any provision for future generations. Previous generations will already either have saved or not saved for them. Either way, it is not in their interest to put anything by for future people. Rawls sees this difficulty. To give the intuitively correct result, he alters the original position by adding ties of sentiment between successive generations. But it is not clear how much saving this *ad hoc* device would generate.

Some critics of Rawls reject the whole model of the original position. Others think that, to deal with this issue, it needs to be altered more drastically, perhaps by including members of every generation among the contractors. But this interpretation has problems of its own. The policies the contractors agree on for conserving or depleting resources may determine how many generations there are. And there is something elusive about a contract agreed by a group whose composition depends on what the contract says.[6] Perhaps not every generation need be represented. It might be enough for contractors to be from different generations, but not know which they belonged to.

The general theories of Hare and Rawls raise too many issues to pursue here. And the equality principle can be supported by reasons which do not require any such theoretical superstructure.

5. Hare discusses this last objection in *Moral Thinking, Its Levels, Method and Point*, Oxford, 1981, p. 15ff.

6. These comments on Rawls derive from Brian Barry, 'Justice between Generations', in P. M. Hacker and J. Raz (eds.): *Law, Morality and Society*, Oxford, 1977; and from D. Clayton Hubin: 'Justice and Future Generations', *Philosophy and Public Affairs* 1976.

One line of thought makes a direct appeal to our intuitive responses, without requiring any complex theory. An imagined bus journey is used by R. and V. Routley to shed light on some of the issues in the nuclear power debate.[7]

The bus carries both passengers and freight on its long journey. It is always crowded, but passengers keep getting on and off, and the drivers change, so that quite different people are on board at different stages of the journey. Early in the journey, a container of highly toxic and explosive gas is put aboard, destined for somewhere near the end of the route. The container is very thin, and the consigner knows it is unlikely to survive the journey intact. If it breaks, some of the passengers will probably be killed. Sending the container of gas on the bus seems an appalling act. The consigner might make various excuses. It is not *certain* the gas will escape. If it does, perhaps the bus will have crashed and killed everyone first. Or perhaps the passengers on the bus at the other end of the journey will be people of a different type who do not mind being killed. He further tries to justify his act by pleading economic necessity: his business will crash unless he sends the container on the bus. The Routleys plausibly claim that none of this adds up to a good defence of the consigner's action. Their intended parallel with the nuclear waste problem we are leaving for future generations does not need spelling out.

There is one defence of the consigner's act whose serious use is almost unimaginable. This is that the harm done does not matter at all, simply because it is done to people who are not on the bus at the time the container is put aboard. Nobody would suppose that getting on at a later stop rather than an earlier one deprived people of any claim to consideration. It may be replied that all the people who get on at later stops are now alive, and so have a claim on us in a way future generations do not. But the supposed importance of this distinction is hard to believe in. Suppose the journey was very long, taking the bus several years, and that the passengers killed by the gas were young children born after consignment. Would this make the act perfectly acceptable?

It may be said that these children have lives overlapping with us. Because we will have relationships with them, they have a claim on our

7. In the best discussion known to me of practical issues involving future generations, 'Nuclear Energy and Obligations to the Future', *Inquiry* 1978.

concern. This argument, if accepted, suggests that, while we must not harm the children of those now alive, we could quite legitimately leave a time bomb which would kill or maim some of *their* children. Or, if we do not want our own children to be upset, we could leave the bomb, not for their children, but at least for their grandchildren or great-grandchildren. To make this point is not merely to use a slippery slope argument, to show the difficulty of drawing the boundaries this kind of view requires. Many perfectly defensible views require boundaries with some element of arbitrariness. The time-bomb case is designed to suggest that the attempt to draw boundaries is mistaken in principle. It is terrible if people are killed or maimed. Whether the bomb was set before the date of their birth, or how long before, is quite irrelevant to our condemnation of the act. Our response suggests that people's moral claims are not reduced by when they live, any more than they are by where they live. And that is the equality principle.

3 Some Views Incompatible with the Equality Principle

There are several influential attitudes to ethics which clash with the equality principle. One is contractarianism. Another is what is sometimes called the 'person-affecting' view. And another is a cluster of approaches which limit claims on us to people with whom we feel natural sympathy or identification.

Contractarianism is a powerful analysis of morality. When our moral thinking reaches the adult stage, and claims about right and wrong are no longer based on appeals to authority, whether parental or religious, there is a problem about what they *are* based on. And there is a prior problem of explaining what they can mean. Contractarianism answers both these problems by saying that we invent right and wrong.[8] We have a common interest in keeping society afloat, and moral rules, resulting from tacit agreements, serve this function. There is an empirical version of contractarianism, which says that this is how the moral rules of various societies did in fact develop. And there is a rational version, which says that, however existing moral codes are to be explained, the only defensible moral principles are those that would be agreed by people

8. cf. J. L. Mackie: *Ethics: Inventing Right and Wrong*, Harmondsworth, 1976.

striking self-interested bargains with each other. The rational version claims not only to make morality intelligible, but also to explain how we can have a motive for being moral.

A disturbing feature of contractarianism is the way it ties people's moral claims to their bargaining power. Those with weak powers of retaliation may find they are in no position to do the deals which would give them rights and other claims. Old people may be given rights because most of us will one day be old, so we are likely to see such rights as being in our long-term interest. But foetuses, young children and the handicapped have no bargaining power with the rest of us. We have passed the stage of being foetuses or young children, and perhaps the chances of being handicapped are too small to weigh with us in self-interested bargaining. And none of these groups has any threats to bargain with. Aborted foetuses do not retaliate. (I am not here arguing that abortion is wrong. Good reasons can be given for a very liberal position on abortion.[9] What I am arguing is that it is unsatisfactory to say that foetuses have no moral claims *because* we can kill them without fear of retaliation. This approach removes moral prohibitions that protect those who are weak and have little bargaining power. Losers will include foetuses, babies, children, minorities, animals, the poor, the handicapped, and perhaps women.[10])

This feature of contractarianism applies strikingly to future generations. We can affect them, but they cannot affect us. So they have no bargaining power on which to base a contract giving them moral claims. So, on the contractarian view, they have none. Those of us who accept the equality principle think that this issue brings out a deficiency in contractarianism. A tough-minded contractarian might prefer to argue that the equality principle is based on some kind of illusion or error. But he will have to say the same about all those values which are not generated by self-interested bargaining. An explanation of our values loses plausibility, at least as a *complete* account, when it ends up having to explain so many of them away.

A second approach which conflicts with the equality principle is the

9. cf. Michael Tooley: 'Abortion and Infanticide', *Philosophy and Public Affairs* 1972.

10. This objection to contractarianism does not apply to the version developed by Rawls, where those striking the self-interested bargain are ignorant of whether or not they belong to one or more of these vulnerable groups. But we have seen that this version has problems of its own in dealing with future generations.

view that all moral beliefs should take a 'person-affecting' form. Impersonal principles may tell us to promote health or happiness, or to eliminate poverty, war or unhappiness. But 'person-affecting' principles tell us to make people healthier or happier, or to rescue people from being poor, being victims of war, or being unhappy. On the person-affecting view, an action is only right or wrong where there are people who are better or worse off than they would have been on some alternative.

At first sight, the distinction may seem purely scholastic. How can we promote health without making people healthier? In most contexts this response is right. But in some cases there is a big difference. And the issue of future generations is such a case. As Derek Parfit has pointed out,[11] different social policies lead to different people being born. Many of us have parents or grandparents who would not have met but for a world war, or but for a decision to build a university or college somewhere. And it is likely that opting for one economic policy or energy policy rather than another will largely or entirely change the composition of a future generation in a country. If so, it will not be possible to say of the members of that generation that they are better or worse off than *they* would have been had the other policy been chosen. For, had it been chosen, they would not have been.

Person-affecting principles seem attractive. They express our sense that people are the centre of value. And impersonal principles convey an air of treating people merely as means to the production of abstract entities such as Health or Happiness. They also seem to have disturbing consequences avoided by person-affecting principles. If our principle is 'maximize happiness', one way of doing this is to create extra people who will be happy. Those repelled by this may prefer the person-affecting principle 'make people happy', which does not have this implication.

But it is a feature of any moral system containing *only* person-affecting principles that such a system gives generations beyond the immediate future little or no claim on our concern. There will probably

11. 'Future Generations: Further Problems', *Philosophy and Public Affairs* 1982. My discussion of person-affecting views derives from Parfit's ideas. Person-affecting views are advocated by Jan Narveson: 'Utilitarianism and New Generations', *Mind* 1967, and in his book *Morality and Utility*, Baltimore, 1967, pp. 46–50. They are also defended in an interesting unpublished paper by Eric Rakowski: 'Obligations to Actual and Potential Persons'.

be no people in distant generations who would exist whichever policy we choose. Where there are no people able to claim they are better or worse off than they would have been, we are considering generations which purely person-affecting systems give no moral claim on us. As with contractarianism, there is a direct conflict with the equality principle. The supporter of such a system will reject the equality principle. And those of us against killing even our remote descendants will find purely person-affecting systems inadequate.

A third approach which conflicts with the equality principle stresses that moral claims are rooted in our natural responses and in our ability to identify with other people. If we had no capacity to feel sympathy with others, or none of the imagination needed to see things from their point of view, it is hard to see how we could be motivated by anything except our own narrowly self-interested desires. Morality influences us because of its roots in our emotional life. Some of these emotional reactions may be explained by the evolutionary usefulness of the behaviour they promote, while some may have their origin in the social conditioning which helps hold human communities together. But, whatever the balance of genetic and environmental factors in a particular case, the importance of these responses in motivating altruism is hard to deny.

The suggestion is that we do not have any natural feelings of affection or concern for people living in two hundred years' time. And, because we do not identify with them, we have no reason for being motivated by consideration of their interests.

We can accept that our emotional responses play a key role in the development of our moral beliefs. We do not have to accept the supposed consequence that our values can never go beyond these natural responses. It is possible for thought to cast doubt on some of the moral boundaries which come naturally to us. We care more about a friend injured in a car crash than about thousands of people killed or injured in an earthquake at the other end of the world. But we may not trust this difference of response as a good guide to what should be done. And this applies equally to our relative lack of identification with people living in the future. Our lack of concern seems caused by our limited imagination: the bias towards here and now. When we think critically, we realize that distant people (in place or time) *would* evoke our concern if we could meet them. So our indifference can be seen as a kind of illusion of

147

perspective: a limitation we should try to overcome. It may have been harmless in the Stone Age, but now we often have to take decisions affecting people remote from us. And it is not obvious that our intuitive feelings of distance are a better guide to action than the equality principle.

4 Practical Constraints on the Equality Principle

There are obvious practical constraints. We often have a fair idea of the likely effects of our actions on people now alive. But our confidence goes down steeply when we are thinking instead about our impact on the lives of people in two hundred years' time. We may decide to use genetic engineering to raise their IQ, only for it to turn out that *this* set of intellectual skills is largely irrelevant to dealing with their problems. Or we may conserve fossil fuels without anticipating scientific advances making them unnecessary. Or, alternatively, what we leave our descendants may be the cause of quarrels and wars which would otherwise be avoided. The limits of practical predictability need no emphasis.

These limits do not only apply to predicting the long-term consequences of what we do. They also apply to predictions about the tastes and values of future people. We may be a bit sceptical about how far people in the eighteenth century could have anticipated what things we find desirable. But, with the possibility of genetic and neurobiological technologies being applied, we have reason for being even more doubtful about how far the outlook of our descendants in two hundred years will be like ours.

It is possible to exaggerate these limits to prediction. The Routleys have warned of this:

We do have excellent reason to believe, especially if we consider 3,000 years of history, that what people there are in a hundred years are likely to have material and psychic needs not entirely unlike our own, that they will need a healthy biosphere for a good life; that like us they will not be immune from radiation; that their welfare will not be enhanced by a high incidence of cancer or genetic defects, by the destruction of resources, or the elimination from the face of the earth of that wonderful variety of non-human life which at present makes it such a rich and interesting place.[12]

12. op. cit., p. 154.

The Routleys here make a strong case for the view that we have good reason to avoid inflicting on future generations things that we now would regard as a disaster. The claim that our descendants might not mind any nuclear radiation, cancer or genetic defects resulting from our nuclear waste policy does sound like the kind of feeble excuse given for sending the container of gas by bus.

When considering our powers of prediction it seems plausible to say two things. Our views on how to give our descendants a good life *may* be roughly right, but are very likely to be wildly wrong. Our views on what would bring disaster to our descendants *may* be wrong, but are very likely to be roughly right. If these two points are correct, it seems that the equality principle has strong implications for the issue of nuclear waste, but weaker implications for attempts to enhance the lives of future generations.

5 Against Utopias

Future generations are unlikely to share all our values. One obvious consequence of this is that we should not plan utopias for them.

Utopian planning, even when intended for the immediate future, has been much criticized. Utopias are always tidy and boring. They reflect the imaginative limits of their creators. One critic has said that 'no utopia has ever been described in which any sane man would on any conditions consent to live, if he could possibly escape'.[13] And the drawbacks are even clearer when we think of plans aimed at several generations ahead. John Mackie, arguing once in a discussion against some optimism of mine, said that if the Victorians had been able to use genetic engineering, they would have aimed to make us more pious and patriotic.

So, while we should be concerned to avoid harm to future generations, we should avoid utopian designs for their lives. We need to remember the limitations of our own outlook. This is a reason for valuing what Karl Popper, in his criticisms of utopianism, called the 'open society':

13. Alexander Gray: *The Socialist Tradition*, New York, 1968, quoted in Robert Nozick: *Anarchy, State and Utopia*, New York, 1974. Support for Alexander Gray's view can be found in F. E. Manuel: *Utopias and Utopian Thought*, Boston, 1966.

one where, even at the level of fundamental values, criticism and the possibility of change are kept alive.

6 In Defence of Intervention

The drawbacks of utopianism are familiar and obvious. But it is often too readily thought that these drawbacks show the truth of the negative view: that we should limit our planned influence on future generations to the avoidance of disasters for them. (A narrow version of this view is that our sole concern should be that we do not *cause* such disasters: we must not be the people who leave the container of gas on the bus. A broader version says that we should also, where possible, help future generations avoid disasters not of our making.)

This negative view of our concern for the future closely resembles what Karl Popper has called 'piecemeal social engineering'.[14] He says,

The politician who adopts this method may or may not have a blueprint of society before his mind, he may or may not hope that mankind will one day realize an ideal state, and achieve happiness and perfection on earth. But he will be aware that perfection, if at all attainable, is far distant, and that every generation of men, and therefore also the living, have a claim; perhaps not so much a claim to be made happy, for there are no institutional means of making a man happy, but a claim not to be made unhappy, where it can be avoided. They have a claim to be given all possible help if they suffer. The piecemeal engineer will, accordingly, adopt the method of searching for, and fighting against, the greatest and most urgent evils of society, rather than searching for, and fighting for, its greatest ultimate good. This difference is far from being merely verbal. In fact, it is most important. It is the difference between a reasonable method of improving the lot of man, and a method which, if really tried, may easily lead to an intolerable increase in human suffering.

Popper's version of the negative view is the broad one: he allows that people have 'a claim not to be made unhappy' *and* 'a claim to be given all possible help if they suffer'. His position relies heavily on two contrasts, neither of them completely sharp. The first is where utopian plans (large-scale, detailed and rigid) are contrasted with the smaller, more flexible measures that count as 'piecemeal engineering'. And there is the contrast between eliminating an evil and promoting a good. Each of these contrasts

14. K. R. Popper: *The Open Society and its Enemies*, Fifth Edition, London, 1966, p. 158.

is a matter of degree, rather than being marked by any clearly determined boundary. (Is a campaign for better schools the promotion of a good, or the elimination of a cluster of evils, such as ignorance and illiteracy?) But, even without sharp boundaries, we are able to understand the two dimensions indicated, and Popper's preference in each case for measures towards one end of the continuum rather than the other.

The difficulty is the extent to which the case for the negative view depends on treating the two contrasts as one. Popper's arguments for the negative view draw on the defects of utopianism: perfection is at best distant, and there are no institutional means of making people happy. (This last point about the absence of *institutional* means of increasing happiness might be questioned. Even if true it would be no argument against the possibility of using genetic engineering or brain technology to make people happier.) When we distinguish between the two contrasts, we need not accept Popper's alternatives: either utopianism or only negative intervention. In bringing up children, we may hope to encourage their talents, or their curiosity and imagination, in ways we hope will enrich their lives, without trying to realize some blueprint of the ideal life for them. It needs to be argued, rather than just assumed, that the same kind of non-utopian but positive policy is impossible at the social level. If genetic engineering or other techniques can be used to produce future generations who transcend our limitations, whether physical, intellectual or emotional, the case against utopianism need not rule this out. For, as argued earlier about genetic engineering, there need be no plan for an ideal type of person drawn up by some committee. And we can recognize that our great-grandchildren will live by their values rather than ours, without as a result wishing to confine them within our own genetic limitations.

7 A Possible Conflict

If the argument of this chapter is right, people of future generations have in principle claims on our concern just as great as people now alive. Where the avoidance of disaster for them depends on what we do, this should have the same weight as if the disaster were to people now. Our restricted ability to make accurate long-term predictions, together with the probability of changes of outlook, set limits to programmes designed

151

to confer positive benefits on future people, but some positive programmes of this kind may be worth attempting. As biotechnology increases our power to influence what people are like, different positive programmes may become possible. And where we can choose between them, there may be a conflict between two underlying aims. We could be guided by the aim of making future people happy, perhaps by making sure that their preferences and the kind of world they inhabit are as closely matched as possible. Or we could be concerned to give them the widest possible freedom of choice between different kinds of life. These two aims should now be looked at.

Chapter 12 Adjustment

The problem is to design a world which will be liked not by people
as they now are but by those who live in it. 'I wouldn't like it' is the
complaint of the individualist who puts forth his own susceptibilities
to reinforcement as established values. A world that would be liked by
contemporary people would perpetuate the status quo. It would be liked
because people have been taught to like it, and for reasons which do not
always bear scrutiny. A better world will be liked by those who live in it
because it has been designed with an eye to what is, or can be, most
reinforcing.

B. F. Skinner: *Beyond Freedom and Dignity*

Out of the crooked timber of humanity no straight thing was ever made.

Immanuel Kant

If we have effective techniques both of behaviour control and of genetic
engineering, some will be tempted to put them together to make future
generations happier. One form of this temptation is the utopian plan of
harmonizing desires and the world. B. F. Skinner says the problem is
to design a world that will be liked by those who live in it. The utopian
plan goes one stage further. It adjusts both the world *and* people's desires
until they are in harmony. (Skinner's own aim involves adjusting people
too, as a large part of the 'world' we like or dislike is other people.) Two
suggestions made here go against all this. We should not plan utopias
because future people will not share our outlook. And the use of
conditioning, drugs or brain stimulation in the utopian plan would
deprive us of control over the sort of people we are. Our project of self-
creation would be destroyed.

Genetic engineering allows a possible response to both these criticisms.
The objection to utopianism is met by designing not only utopia but
also people who will like it. And the objection to external moulding of

our desires and behaviour is met by designing people who place no value on self-creation. Combining genetic and environmental technology (the Brave New World strategy) in this way generates a kind of defence of the utopian project.

Many of us feel a strong resistance to this strategy of utopian adjustment. It arouses in extreme form the opposition we now feel to 'personnel management' and other present types of manipulation. We have the thought that, while social harmony may be desirable, it is better to take people as they are than mould them to fit. We should adjust society to people rather than people to society. But this thought is vague. When looked at more closely, it turns out to have several distinct components. One strand of thought is resistance to the idea of changing human nature at all: a form of conservatism which has been rejected here. Another reason for opposition depends on beliefs about the quality of different kinds of life. And a further line of thought is that autonomy and self-creation have a kind of importance not recognized in the utopian's reply about designing people who do not care about them.

1 Quality and the Satisfaction of Desires

We do not have to accept some general principle of conservatism about human nature in order to resist the utopian plan of adjustment. Our objection may be different. Suppose we are offered a future in which self-creation and the value placed on it are wiped out. (Perhaps we are offered Brave New World or the life of Sisyphus Mark Three.) We may opt for having fewer of our desires satisfied rather than accept such a loss of quality.

This ties in with more general doubts about treating the satisfaction of desires as the only ultimate social goal. We are very adaptable. Even without biotechnology, we adjust to adverse or dreary circumstances, often by revising downwards our hopes, and by making our desires 'realistic'. This psychological adaptability, which is so useful and even admirable, carries with it the danger that we will settle for a world far less good than we could have. Contentment is not enough.

The danger is that social decisions will be guided by a one-dimensional utilitarianism. On this version, the aim of increasing happiness is interpreted either as increasing the number of satisfied desires, or as reducing the number of unsatisfied ones. (The difference between these two versions becomes important when technology makes it easy to create or eliminate desires.) What makes this version one-dimensional is that desires are considered in isolation, without regard to the person's attitude towards them, or the role they play in his or her life. The importance of desires is simply a function of their strength. One-dimensional utilitarianism seems to give no grounds for resisting a world of people like Sisyphus Mark Three. It seems to have no argument against any version of utopian adjustment, other than contingent and precarious claims about practical obstacles.

It is a strength of utilitarianism that the value of states of affairs is not thought to derive from some mysterious source external to ourselves. For utilitarians, the value of anything depends on its relation to the experiences or desires of conscious beings. Unhappiness and the frustration of desires are to be accepted only where there is a sufficiently compensating benefit to someone. In the absence of conflict with anyone else's interests, the fact that someone wants something is a good reason for his having it. Some of us, although attracted by this linking of value with people's interests, will yet find inadequate any view which offers only practical objections to all schemes of utopian adjustment. We will be pulled both ways when we consider utilitarianism.

If we continue to reject one-dimensional utilitarianism, we have two options. The first is to identify utilitarianism with the one-dimensional version, and to reject it in favour of a pluralist approach to value. This pluralism has been eloquently advocated by Isaiah Berlin:

The world that we encounter in ordinary experience is one in which we are faced with choices between ends equally ultimate, and claims equally absolute, the realization of some of which must inevitably involve the sacrifice of others ... It seems to me that the belief that some single formula can in principle be found whereby all the diverse ends of men can be harmoniously realized is demonstrably false. If, as I believe, the ends of men are many, and not all of them are in principle compatible with each other, then the possibility of conflict – and of tragedy – can never wholly be eliminated from human life, either personal or social. The necessity of choosing between absolute claims is then an inescapable characteristic of the human condition.[1]

1. 'Two Concepts of Liberty' (1958), reprinted in *Four Essays on Liberty*, Oxford, 1969, pp. 168–9. See also Bernard Williams: 'Conflicts of Values', in *Moral Luck*, Cambridge, 1981; James Griffin: 'Are There Incommensurable Values?', *Philosophy and Public Affairs* 1977; Charles Taylor: 'The Diversity of Goods', in Amartya Sen and Bernard Williams: *Utilitarianism and Beyond*, Cambridge, 1982.

The second option is to consider whether a more sophisticated version of utilitarianism will enable us to resist utopian adjustment while preserving the link between value and interests. To do this we need a more complex picture of people's interests than the one-dimensional utilitarian has. This will take account of such things as our concern for autonomy and self-creation. And it will be necessary to recognize that desires do not just vary in intensity, but also vary in the role they play in our lives. We have attitudes towards our desires, and sometimes would not exchange the satisfaction of one for any amount of satisfaction of another. (I like talking to people and I like espresso coffee. But I like talking to people so much more, that no amount of espresso coffee would compensate for having to forgo conversations with some of the people I know. And the elimination of the liking for coffee does not seem a worrying prospect, while I would do a lot to resist any elimination of my pleasure in talking to friends.)

A version of utilitarianism which took adequate account of these psychological complications would not support the obliteration of all desires which could not be satisfied. It could resist the slide to utopian adjustment. In taking account of these other dimensions of our psychology, it would come close to some versions of pluralism.

It might be argued that the one-dimensional utilitarian has been unfairly treated here, and that he too can take account of the psychological complications. His view is that the satisfaction of any desire is good, but that the importance of satisfying desires varies with their strength. He could argue that the reason why autonomy and self-creation are important is that we mind about them so much. The desire to be a person of a certain kind, even one with some unsatisfied desires, may be a very strong one, and so be given great prominence by the one-dimensional utilitarian.

This reply has obvious force. But there are grounds for unease about it. Suppose I am in the power of some behaviour controller, who tells me that he is going to turn me into Sisyphus Mark Three. I reply that this goes against my strongest desire, which is to be a person with powers of self-creation denied to all versions of Sisyphus. But the behaviour controller replies that my future desire to roll stones can be made much more intense than my present desire for self-creation. Where the future desire is stronger than my present desire to be a particular kind of person, and where the future desire is also at least as likely to be satisfied, it is not clear that the one-dimensional utilitarian has any remaining argument against the change.

Many philosophers are sure they know what utilitarianism is, and easily take sides for and against it. But if we find the one-dimensional version inadequate, there is the problem of seeing where the boundary comes between pluralism and more complex kinds of utilitarianism. For the complex utilitarian, there is the problem of defining a stable position, which does not collapse, on one side into the one-dimensional version, or on the other side into something not recognizably utilitarian at all. For the pluralist, there is the problem that, if he admits that his various goods are valuable because we care about them, he has to give an account of caring about things that does not collapse into desiring things. If valuing things is not ultimately different from desiring them, pluralism is in danger of collapsing into complex utilitarianism.

Until the boundary between pluralism and complex utilitarianism is more clearly indicated, those of us in that region may often be unsure on which side of it we are. (And, since there can be different forms of complex utilitarianism, we may be on different sides of the boundary with respect to different versions.) Many of the most interesting disagreements cut across the lines between utilitarians and their opponents. In thinking about biotechnology, complex utilitarians may have more in common with some pluralists than with one-dimensional utilitarians. And what they have in common is something important to defend: the belief that quality often should not be sacrificed to contentment.

2 Autonomy

Another objection to utopian adjustment is on grounds of autonomy. We value being free to decide for ourselves what we are to be like, and what sort of life we will lead. If someone else plans my desires, little room is left for this. Autonomy has been mentioned as an objection to behaviour control, and seems a possible objection to genetic engineering.

It might be said that the genetic supermarket is objectionable on grounds of autonomy. Those who oppose attempts by the state to impose a particular outlook on citizens are often also unsympathetic to parents who try to impose an outlook on their children. Although even the most liberal usually accept that some actions are so harmful to others that

157

parental discouragement or state legislation are necessary, belief in the value of autonomy requires either kind of intervention to be justified.

The onus of argument is on government or parents to show that the harm avoided or the good done is enough to justify the intervention to mould behaviour or character. A system where marriages are arranged by parents may, on grounds of autonomy, be just as objectionable as a system where governments order people to take particular jobs. Parents valuing autonomy will not have some blueprint for their children. The aim will be for the children to decide largely for themselves what sort of people they are to be.

It may seem a natural extrapolation from such attitudes to object that the genetic supermarket gives parents too much power over the lives of their children. But the extrapolation is less justified than it may seem.

One complication here is that those who bring up children unavoidably have a great influence on them. Even if parents intervene as little as possible, or intervene in ways that make the children react against them, their decisions still affect the nature of the children. (This is not to speculate about *how* important, relative to genetic factors, or to other environmental ones, parental influences are. The claim is the modest one that different parental policies have different results.) So parents acting on a belief in autonomy would be unrealistic if they aimed not to influence what their children were like. A more plausible view stresses parental encouragement of autonomy: children being encouraged increasingly to take their own decisions as they grow older. This opposition to people being stifled by being denied choices, or by having their choices overridden, does not depend on the fiction that upbringing has no causal influence.

On this more plausible view, it is acceptable for parents to encourage children to have some desires rather than others. (The acceptability varies according to the desires involved and the means used.) It is also acceptable for parents to encourage children to develop abilities and skills, although perhaps not for them to discourage the development of others.

Applying this to positive genetic engineering, the restrictions generated fall a long way short of a total ban. It is objectionable for parents to choose genes with a view to impairing or eliminating abilities: say, choosing to have children who are unable to read. But it is acceptable, on this view, to increase children's abilities, and to opt for them to have one set of desires rather than another. Reducing their abilities may prevent them from taking decisions or acting on them, while increasing their abilities does not. And autonomy is not violated if we use genetic engineering to give people at the start of life a tendency to have a particular set of desires. This is not different in principle from doing the same thing by education or other environmental influences. It is another way in which parents affect the way their children turn out. But it does not override their autonomy. *That* would require overriding their desires or decisions. At the stage of being genetically engineered, the people or potential people in question have no desires and have taken no decisions.

There are complications here over whether altering desires is quite separate from altering abilities. There are further complications about whether it is possible to increase some abilities without diminishing others. But these complications are problems of parenthood in general, and are not peculiar to genetic engineering. If we feel roughly clear about the distinction between environmental influences which violate autonomy and those that do not, the same line between different genetic influences seems no less clear. And ruling out *all* parental choice of their children's genes is not a consequence of any plausible view about autonomy.

But the autonomy objection does have force against behaviour control, which takes away our ability to shape our own lives. It was argued earlier that this is not just an objection based on the inequality between controllers and others, but applies also to mutual control through a democratically programmed machine. Once our lives are under way, and we have views about how we want them to go, we do not want to be altered according to some external plan, however impersonally devised.

The utopian's reply is that he will design people who do not mind about this objection. But this reply, if accepted, has the alarming property of silencing any objection to anything. We make slavery acceptable by designing people who like being slaves. If we value being in control of our own lives, and find the utopian reply inadequate, we cannot appeal to the frustration and despair caused by lack of autonomy. The utopian has eliminated those drawbacks. We have to say that the value of having an autonomous and self-creating life is independent of them. Autonomy is not of value merely as a means to contentment.

Appeals to autonomy, although of importance here, are not adequate as a complete response to utopian adjustment. It may be tempting, when we hold that autonomy has a value independent of its contribution to

159

contentment, to think that we can eliminate the need for controversial claims about quality of life, and cite autonomy as the sole and decisive objection to utopian adjustment. But this is implausible. Belief in autonomy tells us that people's desires and choices should be respected, but it is silent about influencing which desires people have. Nothing is said about some patterns of desires, with their associated kinds of life, being better or worse than others. Like one-dimensional utilitarianism, belief in autonomy gives us no objection in principle to creating only people who live like Sisyphus Mark Three.

Belief in autonomy usually takes one of two forms. The first version, sometimes known as libertarianism, involves absolute prohibitions on various kinds of interference in people's lives. The idea is often stated in terms of rights: people have the right to take certain decisions for themselves, and to live their lives in their own way. These rights function as side constraints, limiting what others may do in pursuit of their own personal or social goals. The second version treats autonomy as something which should be maximized, rather than as an absolute constraint on what people can do to each other. The difference comes out over the question of whether people should be free to do things which will severely restrict their own future freedom of action. (Examples are taking a highly addictive drug, becoming a nun, selling yourself into slavery, signing up for a long period in the army.) On the libertarian view, no one should prevent anyone doing any of these things. Preventive interference would be a prohibited violation of autonomy. But on the maximizing view, there could be a case for intervention. A breach of autonomy now could secure greater autonomy later.

Neither of these versions on its own provides a satisfactory response to utopian adjustment. The libertarian view seems not to rule out *any* genetic engineering. We could choose to have children who were genetically predisposed to disorders involving pain or mental deficiency. Because we would not be overriding anyone's current preference or decision, libertarianism has nothing to say. A modified version of libertarianism could perhaps escape this by appealing to some broader theory of rights, some of which might be violated by such genetic engineering. But in doing so, libertarianism moves away from appealing to autonomy, and becomes indeterminate until the rights are specified.

The maximizing version of autonomy is almost equally unsatisfactory when taken on its own. It rules out giving a child a genetic disorder involving pain, but only to the extent that pain impairs freedom of action. It rules out genetically engineering mental deficiency on the same basis. But it does not rule out engineering Sisyphus Mark Three, as his narrow life comes from his narrow desires rather than from any limits of his autonomy. Although, in this context at least, the maximizing version is an improvement on libertarianism, neither version is adequate as a full account of what is wrong with utopian adjustment.

The objection on grounds of autonomy is a powerful one, and is not met by the utopian's proposal to design people who do not care about autonomy. But it supplements, rather than replaces, the objection about loss of quality.

3 Neutrality

Another possible argument against utopian adjustment is based on a particular version of liberalism. This view is characterized by the belief that governments should be neutral between different conceptions of the good life.[2] The belief that, other things being equal, we should try to avoid an official government view on what sort of people there should be, was used earlier to argue for many genetic-engineering decisions being decentralized. Subject to certain restrictions, the genetic supermarket may be a better system than having a central policy. It is likely, though not certain, that the genetic supermarket would lead to great variety, and to 'experiments in living' which contribute to the growth of human consciousness.

The importance of autonomy, the desirability of experiments in living, and certain views about treating people as equals, all contribute to the case for governmental neutrality between different versions of the good life. But it is implausible to treat this neutrality as an absolute principle, never to be overridden. There is some departure from neutrality when the genetic supermarket is restricted to prevent parents giving their children what most of us think are serious handicaps. Some of us are pleased that the state departs from neutrality to subsidize education and the arts. We may feel that similar departures from neutrality in genetic policy should not be ruled out absolutely.

2. See Ronald Dworkin: 'Liberalism', in Stuart Hampshire (ed.): *Public and Private Morality*, Cambridge, 1978, and Bruce A. Ackerman, *Social Justice in the Liberal State*, New Haven, 1980.

The case for neutrality between versions of the good life is sometimes held to apply, not just to governments, but to anyone with power over others. Bruce Ackerman has applied this view to parental choice in the genetic supermarket.[3] He argues that parents have no right to use the power given by genetic engineering to mould their offspring in one way rather than another. He thinks that such decisions by any power-holders, whether governments or parents, are objectionable departures from neutrality. His solution is a genetic lottery. from which are excluded only those characteristics that would be considered disadvantageous by every member of the generation already in existence.

Ackerman is clearly correct that severe restrictions on genetic engineering follow from the principle that power-holders should never depart from neutrality. What is less clear is that we should choose to accept these restrictions rather than abandon this sweeping version of the neutrality principle. Some doubts about the principle concern its implications for the quality of life. (This is unsurprising. These considerations, in so far as they are the least controversial, are precisely what the principle aims to exclude.) It raises an obstacle to public support either for the arts or for schools which teach more than those minimal skills which would gain unanimous support in an educational referendum. And, in the case of Ackerman's genetic lottery, it only needs one person who thinks that suffering is ennobling for otherwise unnecessary genetic disorders to be included to blight the lives of future people. Accepting that there is a case for neutrality does not commit us to being neutral at all costs.

4 The Human Zoo

The utopian project offers the tempting possibility of a world where all desires are satisfied. This option, especially when contrasted with our present world, is not easily dismissed. But it conflicts with an alternative aim: that of creating a world with the widest possible choice between different kinds of life. The second aim also appeals to values with a deep hold on us: our enthusiasm for human variety, and our related commitment to autonomy and self-creation. Fortunately, these aims are in partial harmony. Because many of our deepest desires are bound up with auto-

3. op. cit., chapter 4.

nomy and self-creation, *we* are more likely to be satisfied in a world where many alternatives are open. But, with the possibility of creating new types of people, the two aims may come apart. Utopian adjustment may then lead to kinds of behaviour control which go against our belief in autonomy.

But autonomy is not the whole case against utopian adjustment. For, as we have seen, Sisyphus Mark Three does not lack autonomy. If he stops wanting to roll stones, his decision to do something else will not be frustrated. What is wrong with his life has to do with the narrow range of his desires. He may even have a project of self-creation, but one narrowly centred on developing the abilities needed for increasingly stupendous feats of stone-rolling.

Imagine a world, produced by utopian adjusters, which took account of the desirability of autonomy and variety. In one place is Sisyphus, contentedly, and of his own choice, rolling stones. Nearby is someone else, hopping about in complicated patterns. There are thousands of such people. They are spending their lives building towers out of marzipan, writing articles about meaning, knitting huge maps of the moon. They are all autonomous, contented and different. Call this world the Human Zoo. Those of us doubtful about the quality of life there have an objection which is not reducible to questions of autonomy and variety.

The problem is whether this objection about quality can be defended against Skinner's criticism that it is just a prejudice. How far should it be dismissed as the product of biases generated by our present genes and conditioning?

Chapter 13 Perspectives

The upshot of these considerations is that justice as fairness is not at the mercy, so to speak, of existing wants and interests. It sets up an Archimedian point for assessing the social system without invoking *a priori* considerations. The long-range aim of society is settled in its main lines irrespective of the particular desires and needs of its present members.

John Rawls: *A Theory of Justice*

Part of the case for thinking systematically about kinds of life as a whole is that piecemeal decisions may bring about a world much less good than we could create. And there are some aims, attractive in themselves, whose exclusive pursuit can lead to a world less good than is possible. We have seen that one-dimensional utilitarianism does not rule out ways of life with unacceptably low quality. And the simple libertarianism which says we should be concerned *only* with autonomy or liberty is inadequate for a similar reason. Of two worlds with equal liberty, and reached by an equally libertarian route, one could be much worse than the other.

But all these opinions about the quality of different kinds of life raise obvious questions. What is 'quality', and how can judgements of this kind be supported? Is there some Archimedian point, from which the kinds of life in different social systems can be assessed, in the way John Rawls thinks there is for assessing their justice? Or do our views simply reflect the biases of our own genetic nature and our own kind of society?

1 External Perspectives

In the discussion of the simple experience machine, the distinction was drawn between internal and external perspectives. From the internal perspective, life on the experience machine is very satisfactory. But, from our external perspective, we may find it unattractive. And we, with our values and outlook, have to decide about plugging into the machine. The same contrast arises when we consider the contented version of Sisyphus or the other people in the Human Zoo. From the internal perspective such lives are fine, but from our external perspective we may think them utterly futile.

Some philosophers think that these contrasting views from the different perspectives should trouble us more than they do. They suggest that the metaphor of perspectives is available only to those who think that there is some objectively true answer to these questions. David Wiggins, in the context of discussing the contrast between lives that have some meaning and lives that are futile, has made a case for this. He says,

All the different perspectives of a single array of objects are perfectly consistent with one another. Given a set of perspectives, we can recover, if only they be reliably collected, a unified true account of the shape, spatial relations, and relative dimensions of the objects in the array. If we forget these platitudes then we may think it is much more harmless than it really is that the so-called outer and inner perspectives should straightforwardly contradict one another. But there is nothing whatever in the idea of a perspective to license this scandalous idea – no more than the truism that two perspectives may include or exclude different aspects will create the licence to think that the participant and external views, as the non-cognitivist has described them, may unproblematically conflict over whether a certain concern is objectively worth while or not.[1]

This is to take the metaphor of perspective rather too seriously. What the metaphor expresses can be stated in terms of beliefs. Some beliefs distort or omit objective facts. A person unaware that he is on the experience machine may believe that François Mitterrand is showing him a less messy way of eating spaghetti. His belief is just false. But other questions of belief may be different. We may disagree with Sisyphus, thinking that his life is less worthwhile than ours. Yet neither we nor Sisyphus need think we are reporting on different aspects of some objective state of affairs. So it may be wrong to say the conflict is over whether a certain concern is *objectively* worth while or not. And where we are dealing with different commitments and concerns, rather than with unproblematic

1. 'Truth, Invention and the Meaning of Life', *Proceedings of the British Academy* 1976, p. 351. This stimulating, impenetrable and original lecture is relevant to the questions discussed here. Although it deals with very abstract issues, it is written with an intense and scandalized passion, sometimes reminiscent of F. H. Bradley.

questions of fact, the idea of conflict between opinions is not such a scandalous one.

Let us call a way of life that seems satisfactory from the internal perspective 'internally adequate'. Where someone finds a kind of life internally adequate, he prefers it to any alternatives of which he is aware. And he finds it worthwhile in itself. (This last feature is meant to exclude the possibility of the test of internal adequacy being satisfied by a very grim life which is preferred to the only alternatives, which are even worse.) And the point about preference brings out the way internal adequacy is relative to alternatives.

Because ways of life can themselves involve filtering information or moulding people's preferences, we are unlikely to find internal adequacy a sufficient justification for choosing to create a particular kind of world. The experience machine is internally adequate, but we can see losses unknown to the person on the machine. Sisyphus, or an inhabitant of Brave New World, may know everything we know, but the shaping of his desires makes for satisfaction with a way of life we find futile. This is not to say that internal adequacy is of no relevance to justifying a state of affairs. Where there are two worlds, similar in other respects, but one is found satisfying by its inhabitants while the other is not, obviously the internally adequate one has a large point in its favour. But if we resist the view that Brave New World, or the life of a supremely contented Sisyphus, cannot be surpassed, we have to hold that other considerations are relevant, as well as internal adequacy.

2 Quality

In our present world, the limitations of internal adequacy are illustrated by certain kinds of severe mental handicap. Some people with these handicaps have lives which, as far as we can tell, are internally adequate. Such a person may seem very content, having only a few simple and mild desires, which he easily satisfies. And he may have no conception of any different kind of life. Although his life may well be worth living, most of us think it sad that he is so limited by his handicap. Once again, contentment is not enough. We think it better to have a life with some intense desires, and to have a wider range of them, even if a lower proportion can be satisfied ('better to have loved and lost ...').

Should we say that quality is just a matter of the intensity and range of experiences and desires? Consider a machine which gives you thousands of different experiences, each generating a corresponding desire which is then satisfied. It is called the Horror Machine. It starts by banging your head against a wall, so that you have an intense desire for this to stop, which it then satisfies. Next it plunges you under water, giving you an intense desire to surface before you drown, which it then satisfies. Now, it starts to attach electrodes to various parts of your body ...

The whole encounter with the Horror Machine is one we would wish to escape from. The range and the intensity of desires are only two of the dimensions that are relevant. Another dimension is our attitude to them. New desires and their satisfaction only enrich life where we are glad to have them. And, with desires we already have, the importance we place on them or their objects is similarly relevant to assessing their contribution to our lives. I may like many of the satisfactions that are available on the simple experience machine, but still think that *no* amount of them would outweigh losing control over my own life, or losing contact with the real world. There can in this way be a kind of lexical ordering of desires or of aspects of life: a set of priorities perhaps only elicited by hypothetical choices between giving up this aspect or that.

It is well known that John Stuart Mill proposed a test for assessing the quality of different pleasures. He said:

Of two pleasures, if there is one to which all or almost all who have experience of both give a decided preference, irrespective of any obligation to prefer it, that is the more desirable pleasure. If one of the two is, by those who are competently acquainted with both, placed so far above the other that they prefer it, even though knowing it to be attended with a greater amount of discontent, and would not resign it for any quantity of other pleasure which their nature is capable of, we are justified in ascribing to the preferred enjoyment a superiority in quality, so far outweighing quantity as to render it, in comparison, of small account.[2]

It is also well known that Mill's test has been criticized. What counts as being competently acquainted with two pleasures? I enjoy reading people's accounts of their lives. Suppose I read Proust's novel about his life, but much prefer the more straightforward autobiography of Lord Home: 'more facts to the page, and a healthier kind of life'. Proustians

2. J. S. Mill: *Utilitarianism* (1861), chapter 2.

may object that I have not fully appreciated Proust, and so am not competently acquainted with both pleasures. But there is a danger of circularity: that only those making the 'right' choice count as competent.

And there is also a problem about what counts as a 'decided preference'. It cannot just be a matter of the number of times one pleasure is chosen over another. Take the pleasure of reading the classics of philosophy. Imagine a house party consisting of people selected for their credentials as judges of this pleasure (perhaps Sir Alfred Ayer, Sir Peter Strawson, Sir Stuart Hampshire, Sir Karl Popper and Sir Isaiah Berlin). The host (perhaps Lord Quinton) has thoughtfully left in the bookshelves such works as Hume's *Treatise*, the *Critique of Pure Reason*, Spinoza's *Ethics*, *Logik der Forschung*, and *My Past and Thoughts*. But perhaps, at the end of the house party, these books will hardly have been looked at. The most popular reading, after the *Good Food Guide* and some back numbers of *Country Life*, may turn out to have been John Le Carré, P. G. Wodehouse, and a book called *How to Develop a Super Power Memory*. Even if this pattern of choice prevailed for years rather than just for one house party, it would not follow that the pleasures of P. G. Wodehouse are 'more desirable' than those of Spinoza.

But Mill's test need not be interpreted as one of totting up favourable choices. When he says of the competent judges of the more desirable pleasure that they 'would not resign it for any quantity of the other pleasure which their nature is capable of', he may not be thinking of choices on particular occasions but rather of the kind of lexical ordering already mentioned. The distinguished philosophers chose Wodehouse more often than Spinoza but, perhaps, if they had to give up one totally, they would keep Spinoza. If so, reading the classics of philosophy passes the more plausible version of Mill's test (call this the 'elimination test'). Even on this version of the test, there may not be unanimity. One of the eminent philosophers, asked to make the decision after spending the house party reading Wodehouse, may make the 'wrong' choice, on the grounds that Spinoza gives him the pip. So long as only a small minority make the 'wrong' choice, Mill's test is satisfied, as he wisely does not require total unanimity.

Mill's elimination test will obviously often fail to give a simple 'yes' or 'no' to a question about whether one pleasure is of greater quality than another. There will often be questions of interpretation, both of how large a majority is required and of what the non-circular tests of competence are.[3] We are clearly not dealing with a simple and conclusive criterion, but with an account of what evidence makes it more or less plausible to say that one pleasure is of higher quality than another. (And we may want to complicate the picture further by allowing that there are different dimensions of quality to assess. A person who would give up P. G. Wodehouse rather than Hume may still feel that the fact he more often reads Wodehouse reflects *something* about the quality of Wodehouse, and so it may be a mistake to concentrate entirely on the elimination test, to the exclusion of considering other evidence from the general pattern of choice.)

When we interpret the elimination test, not as a simple criterion of quality, but as one central source of evidence in support of claims about quality, it is an attractive proposal. If we are to make comparisons of quality at all, it is unsatisfactory not to be able to give supporting reasons. Any single test purporting to give precise and conclusive answers seems unlikely to persuade. But it is also perverse to treat as quite irrelevant the views of those who have experienced (and apparently appreciated) both pleasures. So, when Mill's test for quality is applied in a suitably modest and flexible way, the evidence it provides gives some basis for qualitative comparisons.

3 Bias

If internal adequacy is not enough to show that a kind of world is one we should opt for, it is tempting to say that the choice should be decided by *our* attitudes, when we view different worlds from our external perspective. We prefer privacy to transparency, or the ordinary world to the dreamworld and so, however internally inadequate they might prove to be, we can reject these alternatives in favour of a world more like our own. But this view looks like mere conservatism, unless we can give reasons for thinking that the changes would involve some loss of quality. And, when we try to give reasons, we are pulled towards something like Mill's elimination test. If we try to apply the test in these cases, our status as competent judges may be questioned, in view of our lack of any experience of the new world being considered. This brings out a

3. The problems are discussed by Vinit Haksar, in *Equality, Liberty and Perfectionism*, Oxford, 1979, chapter 11.

more general limitation of the test when we use it to compare the quality, not of isolated pleasures, but of whole kinds of life.

Consider a debate between supporters and opponents of a policy of modernizing a primitive country, lived in mainly by tribal farmers. In such debates, opponents of modernization (sometimes the farmers themselves, sometimes anthropologists) argue that the majority do not want their pattern of life disrupted, and would not choose to live in towns and work in factories. But on the other side it may be argued (perhaps by economists) that industrialization will provide resources for modern education and medicine, whose benefits the tribal people cannot now understand. The argument may be that, when they have fully experienced the benefits, they will be glad of the change.[4] Or, it may be argued that, even if those whose outlook has been moulded by tribal life will always hanker after it, their children will feel no regrets. Suppose the economists' stronger claim is true: that those who undergo the transition will prefer the industrialized state. They have experienced both states, and prefer the second. Does this mean that Mill's test is satisfied?

There are grounds for doubt. Perhaps their judgement is biased, either by social pressures not to seem out of date or reactionary, or by a reluctance to admit mistakes, or by a tendency to make tne best of things? This doubt applies equally if their preference is for their old tribal life. Their judgement may be biased by nostalgia, or by the tendency to think the grass is greener on the other side. This suggests that we require not only competent judges, but also controls against various kinds of bias. To compare life in Switzerland with life in Austria, it would be necessary to ask some who had emigrated one way and some who had gone the other way. Only if there were a solid majority for one country among both groups would we start to have evidence in support of the superiority of that way of life. (Even here we only *start* to have evidence, because of the possibility of other biases. Olaf Stapledon's 'mental malnutrition and poisoning' may be affecting us. Perhaps the newspapers and television in one country support the government, while in the other they oppose it. In the one, they pour out stories of optimism and cheer, while in the other they are filled with gloom and denigration.)

4. This line of argument has been criticized by Jon Elster, in *Ulysses and the Sirens*, Cambridge, 1979, pp. 77–86, and he discusses arguments of this sort applied to the Industrial Revolution in England in 'Sour Grapes – Utilitarianism and the Genesis of Wants', in A. Sen and B. Williams: *Utilitarianism and Beyond*, Cambridge, 1982.

Let us stipulate a version of Mill's elimination test which has built into it controls for bias produced by a person's present position. Call it the 'symmetry test'. Using this test, we have evidence that one state of affairs is qualitatively superior to another where those with experience of both prefer it to the other, whichever state they are in. The state of not having a headache would pass the test when compared with the state of having one. The problems of applying the test in less easy cases are serious, and so we will often (perhaps usually) obtain less than a clearcut answer. In such cases, the test will function as an idealization, in the light of which we assess evidence of varying persuasiveness.

Take the comparison between our own world and the world where our thoughts and feelings are transparent to others. In the ideal case, some of us make the shift to the transparent world, and at the same time a group brought up in the transparent world moves to our world. And, in this ideal case, the preferences are symmetrical: *both* groups overwhelmingly prefer the same world. In practice, the results are unlikely to be so clearcut. There are difficulties, both moral and practical, about carrying out the experiment of bringing up people with no privacy of mind. (The moral problems might be less serious if we had good reason to think their lives would not be made less good, but this is what the experiment is needed to establish.) Perhaps those making the transition to transparency would loathe it at first, but come decisively to prefer it. There is room for different interpretations here. Are they becoming better judges, as they leave embarrassment and inhibition behind? Or are the social pressures of transparency creating a conforming cheerfulness about their state? And if people from the transparent world think our world is worse, is this a powerful piece of evidence? Or should we say that, because of their upbringing, they have never learnt to appreciate the subtleties given to relationships by ambiguity and obliqueness?

Where we compare two kinds of life, and find impressive evidence that one passes the symmetry test, we have a good reason for thinking it qualitatively superior to the other. And when we find evidence that our own preference for a way of life does not have the support of the symmetry test, we have grounds for wondering whether our attitude is the result of some bias.

Take the case of the dreamworld. Suppose that, from our external perspective, we regard the limits of the dreamworld as claustrophobic, and have a decisive preference against any permanent move into it. But

171

consider those who have entered an 'open' version of it, where they are not deceived about its nature and can remember our ordinary world. Suppose they do not share our attitude, but say they are overwhelmingly glad to have made the transition? The possibility is easier to imagine if we vary the example. Suppose *we* are told that our ordinary world is a dreamworld, causally dependent on some quite different state of affairs. Would we be desperate to leave the world we are used to, and to make contact with 'reality'? I would like to find out a bit more before deciding. ('You are one of thousands of humans standing packed together in a small battery, being reared for food on a Martian farm. Martian laws against cruelty to animals require the farmer to provide you with access to a dreamworld.') If things were very bad, I would stay here.

Go back to the case where our world is the causally fundamental one, and where those who have entered the open dreamworld are glad to have done so. They understand our objections about claustrophobia and the lack of scientific research, as well as our doubts about dreamchildren. But, from their point of view, the advantages easily outweigh the draw-backs. And suppose that it is not easy to explain away their preference by citing factors that may bias their judgement. It is then reasonable to ask whether our resistance to the dreamworld is exaggerated, as a result of a conservative bias against what has not been experienced.

At this point, we might be persuaded that our resistance to the dream-world is the product of bias or unfamiliarity. This could result from our scrutinizing our own opposition more closely, perhaps with the help of 'reverse' examples, where our ordinary world turns out to be a dream-world. Or people in the dreamworld (who have turned from it briefly to communicate with us) may persuade us that their choice is based on substantial advantages, by making an impressive case that their preference coexists with a thorough appreciation of our objections and doubts. If our opposition is undermined, we may ourselves decide to enter the dreamworld. Or, we may prefer to stay in the ordinary world, while accepting that this is the result of bias in favour of the familiar. But to accept this is to remove all serious objections to the view that the dreamworld may be better for our descendants. The supporters of the dreamworld, while not altering our choice, will have won the argument for the future.

But our investigations may go the other way. We may think that we understand their case for the dreamworld at least as well as they understand our case against it, and that they are as likely as us to be biased. The fact that our preference does not pass the symmetry test raises the question of bias, but does not in itself establish that it is biased or irrational.

There is more than one way in which a preference may fail to pass the test. In one kind of failure, the test gives a strong support to the alternative preference. (Someone who has never seen colour television may prefer to stay with black and white. But the symmetry test gives strong support to colour if almost all those who have experienced both prefer colour, whichever they now have, and if there is no evidence of biases affecting their judgements. This creates a presumption that the preference for black and white is itself the product of bias or lack of experience.) But other ways of not passing the symmetry test create no presumption about a preference. There may be no decisive view among those questioned in either of the two states. Or there may be asymmetry, where those in one state exhibit a clear preference, and those in the other have the opposite preference. In the case of asymmetry, neither preference passes the test, and so no presumption is created for or against either.

The symmetry test resembles Hare's universalizability or Rawls's original position, in being a device which can be used to identify and correct the effects of bias. But the use of such devices presupposes that our values include commitment to some degree of impartiality. Someone with no such concern can say to Hare that he is not interested in making moral judgements, and can say to Rawls that he is not interested in justice. I am assuming here that we intend claims about the relative quality of different kinds of life to be more than expressions of *any* preferences we happen to have. These claims about quality may be empty if they are in no way linked to anyone's actual or hypothetical preferences. But some preferences and attitudes (not liking a kind of food you only tried when ill, liking some music because it reminds you of someone) seem so much the product of biasing circumstances that no claims about quality can plausibly be based on them. Someone with no such scruples will say confidently that any world he dislikes is of poor quality. The rest of us may be willing to detach judgements of quality from our own preferences where the evidence is that the symmetry test gives strong support to alternative preferences.

But, even when we have a commitment to correct for bias, the symmetry test allows only a partial detachment from our own point of view.

Its results are inconclusive in some cases, including all cases of asymmetry. And it cannot be applied where the comparison needed is not between person A in states X and Y, but between person A in state X with person B in state Y. (Questions about genetic engineering may, often, be of this kind.) And the symmetry test will never tell decisively against states of affairs (such as Brave New World) where people's preferences are adjusted to favour their present position. So even apart from the extent to which the symmetry test is an idealization, its application has severe limitations.

It may be thought that other tests could be devised for ranking worlds in order of quality, in ways that would not be subject to these limitations. But it seems at least equally likely that, when faced with many choices, even our most satisfactory tests would still be silent or inconclusive. If so, the reasons guiding these choices will have to appeal to our 'uncorrected' values and preferences.

4 Archimedes and Neurath

We may be glad that our own way of life is not restricted within limits set by medieval people. And we can see how our descendants might find the limitations of our outlook equally cramping. For this reason, we might welcome the discovery of an Archimedian point, such that 'the long-range aim of society is settled in its main lines irrespective of the particular desires and needs of its present members'.

In ethical writings, appeal is often made to 'moral intuitions': our varied responses of approval or disapproval of actions or states of affairs. Theories about what we should do are criticized on the grounds that they generate intuitively unacceptable decisions. In this book various possible theoretical approaches to the use of biotechnology have been rejected on the basis of intuitive unacceptability. But how sacred are these intuitions? On a favourable view, where intuition and theory conflict, theory has to give way. On a hostile view, intuitions are just a set of prejudices derived from a particular upbringing, and they should be discarded where they conflict with a well-grounded theory.

The anti-intuitive view can be harnessed to various different theories. It may be claimed, as by R. M. Hare, that analysis of moral language gives an acceptability test for moral beliefs, independent of intuitions.

Or it may be said that a contractarian account of morality is the external test. This view dismisses intuitions which do not have the backing of the actual or hypothetical contract.

Strong versions of the anti-intuitive view are implausible. Its supporters normally propose theories that do accommodate many of our intuitive values. But a strong version leaves open the possibility that most, or even all, of our intuitive values might be incompatible with the favoured theory, and so have to be discarded. The theory would be the Archimedian point from which the whole world of values could be moved. But we could surely be justified in choosing to revise or bypass the theory, rather than change our whole attitude to life. (A person might say, 'Some things are more important than the terms of the hypothetical contract,' or, 'If that is the language of morals, then "morals" turns out not to be what I am interested in.')

The Archimedian point from which our intuitions can be criticized seems to require viewing all our attitudes from an external perspective. But is making judgements from a perspective that excludes *all* our attitudes intelligible?

The doubt about the intelligibility of this approach can be illustrated by one traditional proposal. Religious believers have thought that God's position is the Archimedian point. For them, there are the familiar difficulties of showing that God exists and showing that they know what God's views are. But there is the further problem of showing that He is not just one of Us. Why should God's opinions carry such weight? Because He made us as part of His plan? (Suppose a king and queen, rather disliking children, only have a baby to keep the royal line going. The prince grows up wanting to be a psychoanalyst. Suspecting the two jobs might be awkward to do together, he decides not to be a king. 'But you have got to accept the throne. Your being king was our only reason for having you.' 'Oh, I see. That makes all the difference.') What would count as showing that our values should be adjusted to fit God's? What does it mean to say that His are the 'correct' ones? Correct by what standards? And how are *those* standards validated?

Perhaps the idea of judging from an Archimedian point external to our own concerns and commitments is unintelligible. This may seem to suggest that our attitudes cannot rationally be criticized or modified. But this is too brisk.

The pro-intuitive view says that ethical theories have no basis other than intuitions. These theories are an attempt to give a coherent account of our values, which are only revealed by our responses to things. And theories must be controlled and corrected by these responses, in a way that resembles the relation between theory and observation in science.

A strong version of the pro-intuitive view generates an extreme conservatism towards current attitudes. If theory has no power to modify our responses, it is reduced to cataloguing them. Philosophical thought about values becomes a matter of searching for the precise statement of what is already believed and felt. But this strong version is implausible in a way that can be brought out by taking up the parallel with science. It is a familiar point that a theory in science is not just a catalogue of observations. Observations modify theories, but theories modify our interpretation of observations. And where theories conflict with observational reports, we do not in all cases abandon the theory. We often have a range of options to consider, including attributing the observation to error or to some distorting factor not controlled for. Similarly, in thinking about values, it is not obvious that we should adopt the policy that intuitions are all to be taken as fixed points to which theories must be adjusted. One doubt about this is whether our unmodified intuitions are consistent with each other. Another problem is whether the 'moral intuitions' that have such authority are clearly marked off from other likes and dislikes which are not so sacrosanct. And, as we have seen, some of our values may be modified by evidence that they result from some bias.

In epistemology and philosophy of science, few now deny the mutually modifying interaction of theory and observation. It is not plausible to treat all observational reports as sacred. Nor is it plausible to defend the 'Archimedian' approach of Descartes, who tried to combine scepticism about our whole system of beliefs with rebuilding the system from some external vantage point. Philosophers often express what is wrong with this, by quoting Neurath's image of science and philosophy: we are like a sailor who must rebuild his boat at sea. Perhaps each part must be rebuilt, but at each point enough of the boat must be left to keep it afloat.

Neurath's image seems suitable for values too.[5] We do not just have a series of unrelated gut-reactions to things. If we have the degree of reflectiveness needed for a minimally coherent life, our attitudes display

5. I first heard it applied to values by Bernard Williams in a discussion.

some system of priorities. This system may be partly conscious and may, on examination, turn out to be in various ways limited or inconsistent. In rebuilding the system, we must always keep part of it afloat. But only a person of remarkable natural consistency (or remarkable natural self-confidence) will be sure that no reconstruction is necessary.

In taking decisions that will affect the lives of future people, we are bound to be guided by our values. If there is no Archimedian point, this is inevitable. But we will not just create people who repeat our outlook. This is because our values are open-ended. They include a belief in trying to transcend our own biases and limitations. They also include a belief in people creating themselves and so contributing to the unplanned development of consciousness.

Chapter 14 Some Conclusions

The fateful question for the human species seems to me to be whether and to what extent their cultural development will succeed in mastering the disturbance of their communal life by the human instinct of aggression and self-destruction.

Sigmund Freud: *Civilization and its Discontents*

We may insist as much as we like that the human intellect is weak in comparison with human instincts, and be right in doing so. But nevertheless there is something peculiar about this weakness. The voice of the intellect is a soft one, but it does not rest until it has gained a hearing. Ultimately, after endlessly repeated rebuffs, it succeeds. This is one of the few points in which one may be optimistic about the future of mankind ...

Sigmund Freud: *The Future of an Illusion*

It has been suggested here that some things – self-development and self-expression, human contact, being part of the open-ended development of human consciousness – are of central importance to us. At least, this is so when we are sufficiently removed from misery to care what our lives add up to. But much of the misery in the world, which *could* be avoided, will not be eliminated in any of our lifetimes. To someone lacking food, clean water or medical care, or to someone facing torture or caught up in a war, concern with these more subtle values may seem frivolous. (Imagine a town where a flood makes most people homeless, and the few living on high ground go on discussing improvements to their own houses.)

Yet the more urgent concerns do not make the other ones unimportant. People should be rescued, but it also matters what happens to them afterwards. In a world with so much avoidable disaster, it can seem frivolous to be a novelist or a musician, or to work on the foundations of mathematics or on the origins of the universe. It is right to reply that these activities are worthwhile in themselves. But another reply is also relevant. By such choices, people keep alive traditions more fragile than we often think. It has been argued that future generations have some claims on us. One such claim is that we should pass on these traditions, and not let 'the conversation of mankind' fade out. (It is not enough to rehouse those who lose their homes in the flood, if all that remains for them afterwards is life working in an insurance company.)

It is hard to get the right balance between immediate and long-term problems. To ignore the urgent problems is to allow terrible things we could help to avoid. But it is not always wrong to give priority to the further future: at the time of a deadly epidemic, it may be right for *some* doctors to carry on with basic research. And to ignore the subtle values can be philistine and stifling. If we do ignore them, we may leave our descendants a world where the life of a contented consumer is the best any of them can expect.

Perhaps positive genetic engineering in humans will be stopped by insurmountable practical barriers. Perhaps the same is true of the envisaged applications of neurobiology. And it may be found that much of our work is beyond the scope of any future machines. But we have now little reason for confidence in the existence of these technological barriers. It seems worth considering the transformation of human life these developments would bring. If we allow them to take place, people will not stay as they are. In deciding which changes to encourage and which to resist, we need some view about the strengths and weaknesses of our present nature, and some views about what makes for a better or worse life.

1 Transcending Intellectual Limitations

A possible role for positive genetic engineering would be to raise our intellectual capacity. One day, perhaps remote from now, we may start to feel that we are coming up against the in-built limitations of our ability to understand the universe. The Kantian thought that our cognitive constitution may set limits to our grasp of the world is played down in some of the best modern discussions of Kant. But the thought may still be true. It is expressed in a remark I have seen ascribed to J. B. S. Haldane,

179

that the universe may be 'not only queerer than we suppose, but queerer than we can suppose'.

This line of thought is unfashionable because of its associations. In Kant, and in some of the nineteenth-century German metaphysicians who followed him, the stress on the limitations of our sensory and cognitive apparatus was accompanied by the view that we can never know the world as it really is: 'things in themselves' are in principle inaccessible to us, and there is no possibility of our being in a position to say anything about them. Such pessimistic metaphysics cannot easily survive awareness of progress in science. The limitations of our sensory apparatus are real, but we devise instruments to monitor what our unaided senses cannot detect. At any particular time, our scientific theories are imperfect and incomplete. But the fact of scientific progress cannot reasonably be denied. It is hard to see what this progress can be, if not the growth of an increasingly full and accurate understanding of what the world is like. So the realm of unknowable 'things in themselves' is one we are right to dispense with.

But it does not follow from this that our unmodified intellectual equipment is the most that can be needed in extending our scientific understanding of the world. Just as calculus is too much for a dog's brain to grasp, so some parts of physics might turn out to be too difficult for us as we are. No doubt it would be hard to be sure that we were pressing against our limitations. But, faced with a continuing lack of progress on very baffling problems, we might come to suspect this. And we might have some thoughts on what changes in brain functioning could make a difference.

To take this as a possible candidate for positive genetic engineering is not to make the widespread assumption that raising IQ is the obvious change to consider. The relevant intellectual limitations may require deeper changes than merely boosting the cluster of skills measured by IQ tests.

Any programme of genetic engineering to modify our intellectual functioning would obviously have to be very cautious and experimental. But, once it showed signs of working without bad side-effects, it seems likely that some parents would choose to have children who would transcend our traditional limitations. Because our growing understanding of the world is so central a part of why it is good to be human, it would be very tempting for us to break through our genetic intellectual limitations.

If we do have such limits, and do decide to transcend them, our descendants may be glad. To them, our decision might mean escape from a kind of claustrophobia. For the alternative would be to have an understanding of the world that was incomplete yet permanently static. And this kind of stifling is something the human race has not known since we first woke up and started to ask our questions.

2 Emotional and Imaginative Limitations

It may be that we are still far from the limits of our intelligence. Primitive people have brains which, unknown to them, have unused capacity for mathematics and physics. We too may have a great deal of unused capacity. But other kinds of limitation are closer and more obvious. Our limited capacity for altruism, and for the imaginative sympathy it depends on, is one such case.

In optimistic moments, we may hope that our history of cruelty and killing is part of a primitive past, to be left behind as civilization develops. But the events of our own century do not suggest that this process has gone far. We still know large-scale killing, sometimes of the inhabitants of entire cities in war, sometimes extermination of whole peoples as a deliberate policy. We are familiar with the effects of napalm, and not surprised by the daily use of torture in many parts of the world. Less dramatically, but with similar terrible effects, we are used to our own passivity in the face of so much hunger, disease and poverty.

We know all about these things. Because of television, we know about them with more immediacy than was previously possible for those not directly involved. But there is a natural resistance to thinking in general terms about the human limitations these facts display. We switch off the television news and turn to something else. Or we compartmentalize our minds. It is easy to think of each horror as a kind of isolated accident. Vietnam can be explained as due to a series of miscalculations, or Cambodia as the result of the lunacy of Pol Pot, or an Indian famine as the result of a flood or a crop failure. Or, in England, there is the thought that Hitler's policies were carried out by Germans, or Stalin's policies by Communists, neither of whom, of course, are at all like us.

These are all shallow responses. Of course each particular disaster has its own causal explanation. But when they are considered together, it is hard not to see the limitations of human sympathy, and how easily it can be switched off. We acquiesce in avoidable misery. It is possible to speculate that many of us were born with the potential to become torturers, bombers or concentration camp guards. Most people realize other, more desirable potentialities. But there seems as little reason for confidence that, given the same history and circumstances as these people, we would not do the same things. (*Lord of the Flies*, William Golding's response to the Nazi episode, is partly about this.) This is not to say that we should respond to social and political disasters by resigned contemplation of our limitations. We need not accept that acting to make the world a better place is bound to fail. But such action does not have to depend on optimistic illusions about what we are like.

Avoidable evils are not removed, partly because people unaffected do not care enough about them. Thousands of deaths in a faraway country do not stir us like one child run over down the road. Our sympathies are limited and local, with a few close people mattering more than everyone else in the world. This is not altogether bad. We need relationships involving special concern. So it would not be desirable to spread our emotional involvement evenly over the whole human race. But, even making allowances for this, it is hard not to feel that greater capacity for altruism and for concern at a distance would be an improvement. When we think of what we allow to happen, this is not easy to doubt.

This line of thought may be reinforced by thinking again of the Darwinian explanation of how our genes came to be as they are. (Once again, no questions are being begged as to the relative importance of genes and environment. Darwinism explains our *genetic* nature, not our nature.) Our genes are what they are because they were better able to survive than others were. And, to the extent that we are the product of our genes, we are to be explained, in Richard Dawkins's vivid phrase, as survival machines for genes. And, unless we have a very crude form of evolutionary ethic, there is no reason why the qualities we value should exactly coincide with those which have led to gene survival. Perhaps, in terms of our values, the world would be a better place if people were more altruistic and generous than a perfectly calculated survival strategy for genes would make them. It is clear that Dawkins is himself attracted to this view. At the end of his book he says, 'We can even discuss ways of deliberately cultivating and nurturing pure, disinterested altruism – something that has no place in nature, something that has never existed before in the whole history of the world. We are built as gene machines ... but we have the power to turn against our creators. We, alone on earth. can rebel against the tyranny of the selfish replicators.'[1]

If our values favour more altruism than is now best suited to gene survival, we may, as Richard Dawkins suggests, take steps to cultivate it. But, on the Darwinian view, this seems to require either massive control over the environment or else genetic planning. For, in a natural environment, those with more altruism than is best for gene survival will by definition be less successful in propagating their genes than those with the optimal amount. They could be rescued from evolutionary oblivion by drastic social and environmental changes designed to give them a greater chance of survival. But it is hard to see what this would involve, or what other values would be sacrificed. If we cannot make these changes, or else decide the price is too high, the logic of the Darwinian theory is that any genes underlying a tendency to 'surplus' altruism are likely to be eliminated by natural selection. The only alternative would be genetic planning: direct intervention to make sure that the genes we value survive.

Our emotional and imaginative limitations are especially apparent when we consider the psychology of war. We all know how here our technology has grown faster than we have. It is not clear that we will survive at all. Our arrangements for avoiding war are so flimsy, and we have not yet developed the sense of urgency appropriate to our precarious position. Nor have our attitudes sufficiently changed in the ways that would help survival.

It may be that war is the product of particular social arrangements, which could be changed. Perhaps we can change our economic system or our approach to education, or abolish the nation state, without having to change deep aspects of our psychology. And perhaps these social changes will eliminate war. But, given our relative failure so far, we should at least consider the view that the abolition of war may need psychological changes which will not simply follow from political and social reform.

Plausible contributory features of our nature are not hard to suggest. We have a tribal psychology well adapted to survival in the Stone Age. We have the desire to identify with a group; willingness to hate other

1. *The Selfish Gene*, Oxford, 1976, p. 215.

groups; obedience; conformity; aggression; the responses to being part of a crowd; the responses to stirring music, and to uniforms, flags and other symbols; the love of adventure and risk; the need for a simple framework of ideas to make sense of the world; and the desire to believe rather than doubt. These aspects of our nature are not all entirely bad, and they may not contribute equally to war. Some of them may be more easily modified or controlled by social changes than others. But, taken together, they have contributed to the catastrophes we all know. And now they threaten the survival of our species. If either environmental or genetic methods are available, we may be wise to change ourselves if we can.

3 Values and Dangers

If we do decide to change ourselves, taking thought well in advance may help to ensure that the directions we take are guided by our values. The application of science to alter genes or brains may change the shape of human life. With so much at stake, we could not be justified in proceeding without clear aims. This does not imply that there has to be a *single* collective set of goals. As argued earlier, with genetic engineering there is a lot to be said for decentralized decisions realizing a diversity of aims, though subject to some restrictions.

The value we place on diversity may conflict with the goal of eliminating the more harmful and dangerous side of our present nature. This conflict should not be slurred over. It is likely to be a dominant political issue for the first generation to embark on positive genetic engineering.

Whichever way that debate goes, the values guiding it will be those of the decision makers. The objectivity which consists in standing quite outside our own values does not exist. But, even from our own perspective, we can recognize some changes as being for the better. We may have an instinctive conservatism about human nature, but intellectually we can see the links between our psychology and the threats to our survival. The voice of the intellect *is* a soft one, but in some of us, some of the time, it gains a hearing.

We cannot stand quite outside our own values. But it does not follow that we should create for future generations exactly the kind of world we like. Some of the envisaged possible applications of neurobiology are attractive now: perhaps some mood-changing drugs, or some uses of self-administered brain stimulation. Where we resist other applications, we can sometimes recognize and make allowances for the bias of our limited experience and understanding. Perhaps we are glad to have a private inner life, and relieved not to be transparent to other people. We can feel this, and still see that people who had made the transition to transparency might find the gains far greater than the losses. We can make allowances for our own limitations here, and for this reason we may wish to encourage experiments in lowering the barriers of privacy.

In an appropriately cautious way, we should be willing to change what we are like. Some of the dangers are obvious. There are the standard dangers of any new technology: miscalculation and disastrous accidents. And there are the deeper risks of social misuse. These technologies may fall into the hands of governments who aim to enslave people. Or the danger may come from shallow and thoughtless commercial exploitation. People could make profits from selling genetic or neurobiological technology with short-term advantages, without any thought of the world that would result. It needs no emphasis that these dangers are unusually important with the technologies we are considering. Here, accidents or misuse will influence what sort of people there will be.

The other great threat is perhaps less obvious, but I hope it has emerged in this discussion. The danger is that these technologies will be harnessed to a benevolent utopianism which has too crude a view of what life can be. An example is the one-dimensional utilitarianism which aims in a simple way at the maximum satisfaction of desires. A programme based on this outlook could succeed in harmonizing our desires and the world, at the cost of obliterating the self-expressive and self-creative life we now care about. Perhaps it would lock us into the pointless circular activity of the Human Zoo, or put us all on to simple experience machines. In either case, the countervailing desires which come from other perspectives would be eliminated.

One of the worst fears is that we might never escape from these self-perpetuating states. Sometimes, as in certain versions of the experience machine, the programme wipes out all consciousness of other kinds of life. Sometimes it leaves awareness of other possibilities, but wipes out any desire for them. Once we have lost such awareness or desires, there is no certainty they will return. We may have shut down options more valuable than the contentment we have gained. This is a danger which is not confined to crude versions of utilitarianism. It arises with any scheme which has utopian pretensions to finality. It will be avoided if what prevails is belief in human variety and in keeping alive the possibilities of change.

4 Consciousness

The problems we confront now are about ensuring our survival and about eliminating the causes of misery. They will be with us for some time. But, as biotechnology advances, another wave of problems will be upon us. Here a central danger is closing down possibilities: the dreamworld is only an extreme case of this. And this danger may have to be overcome in order to create the perspective from which it can be fully appreciated. (We can see, in a way primitive men could not, how much would have been lost if they had found a drug giving them contentment at the cost of any further intellectual development.)

Our present wave of problems exists partly because modern physical technology has come too early in our social development: before we have outgrown our tribalism and our wars of religion. The parallel danger is that biotechnology will come too soon, and we will shut ourselves into a world more cramping than we need. We may fall into what would seem, from the viewpoint of a more developed consciousness, to be a contented stupor.

John Donne, in one of his sermons, said: 'We are all conceived in close prison, and then all our life is but a going out to the place of execution, to death. Was any man seen to sleep in the cart between Newgate and Tyburn? Between prison and the place of execution does any man sleep? But we sleep all the way. From the womb to the grave, we are never thoroughly awake.'

One claim here has been that consciousness is especially important: that all value derives from contributions to the lives of conscious beings. But it does not follow that pleasurable experience is the only thing of value. A whole life passively consuming pleasure is a narrow one. A broader view of the good life centres on activities and relationships. We mind about the kinds of things we do, and we want to experience things with other people. We also like to think and talk together, sharing and helping to shape each other's responses. In this way we express our-selves, and partly create ourselves and each other. Each of us, to a very small extent, contributes to the development of human consciousness. As a result we, and our descendants, go through life more thoroughly awake.

Index

MORE ABOUT PENGUINS, PELICANS AND PUFFINS

For further information about books available from Penguins please write to Dept EP, Penguin Books Ltd, Harmondsworth, Middlesex UB7 0DA.

In the U.S.A.: For a complete list of books available from Penguins in the United States write to Dept DG, Penguin Books, 299 Murray Hill Parkway, East Rutherford, New Jersey 07073.

In Canada: For a complete list of books available from Penguins in Canada write to Penguin Books Canada Ltd, 2801 John Street, Markham, Ontario L3R 1B4.

In Australia: For a complete list of books available from Penguins in Australia write to the Marketing Department, Penguin Books Australia Ltd, P.O. Box 257, Ringwood, Victoria 3134.

In New Zealand: For a complete list of books available from Penguins in New Zealand write to the Marketing Department, Penguin Books (N.Z.) Ltd, P.O. Box 4019, Auckland 10.

In India: For a complete list of books available from Penguins in India write to Penguin Overseas Ltd, 706 Eros Apartments, 56 Nehru Place, New Delhi 110019.